RUDYARD KIPLING'S

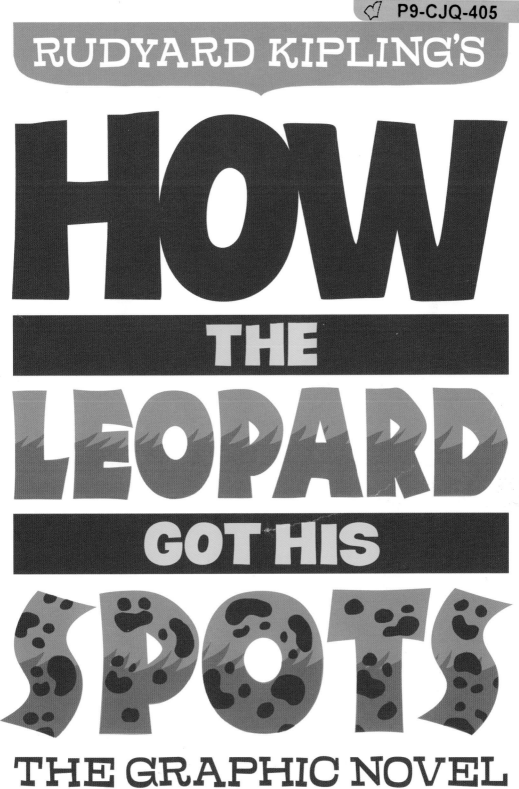

HOW THE LEOPARD GOT HIS SPOTS

THE GRAPHIC NOVEL

Tulien & Rodriguez

STONE ARCH BOOKS • A CAPSTONE IMPRINT

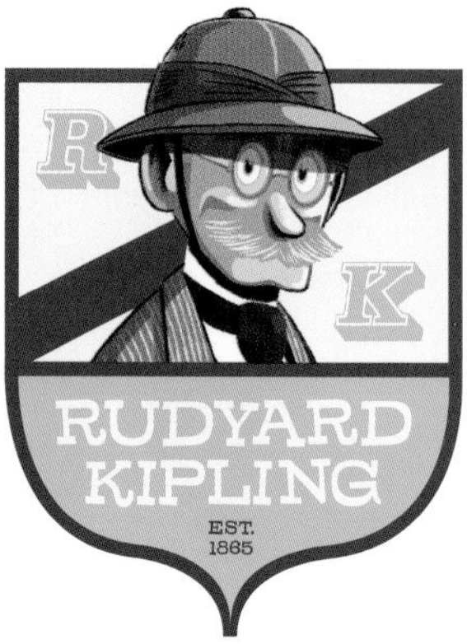
R
K
RUDYARD
KIPLING
EST.
1865

TO OUR READERS

The animal world has long been a place of intrigue. Countless mysteries surround its magnificent creatures. For years, humankind has wondered how animals came to look and act the way they do.

Finally, the questions have been answered. Famed author and worldwide explorer Rudyard Kipling has traveled the globe, searching for the greatest of beasts. He's witnessed and recorded animal behaviors unlike anything seen before. And now he is sharing his findings with the world.

Let Kipling be your guide as you journey into jungles, grasslands, and deserts. Use his invaluable research to unravel the mysteries yourself. It is an exciting time for animal lovers. Thanks to Kipling, we can all be part of it.

Sincerely,
The Editors

HOW THE LEOPARD GOT HIS SPOTS

RUDYARD KIPLING

1 RESEARCH — 04

2 KIPLING'S OBSERVATION — 06

3 CONCLUSION — 34

4 LEARN MORE — 36

5 MEET OUR TEAM — 38

ALSO FROM RUDYARD KIPLING — 40

RESEARCH

SPECIMEN:
SAND-SHADED LEOPARD
(Fig. A)

HABITAT: Sub-Saharan Africa (Fig. B)
HUNTING PARTNER: The Ethiopian (Fig. C)
PREY: Zebra (Fig. D); Kudu (Fig. E);
        Giraffe (Fig. F)

A

Insatiable appetite

Dull, sandy coat

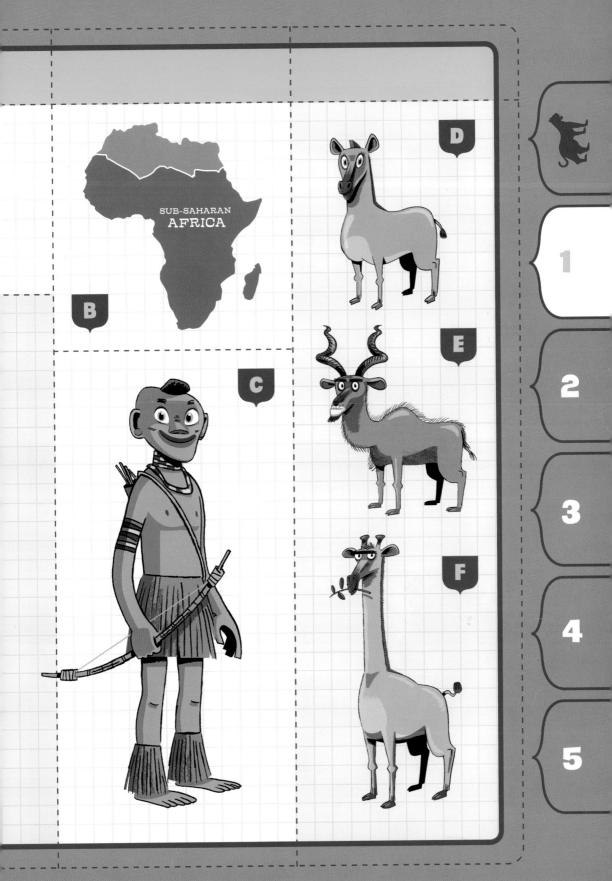

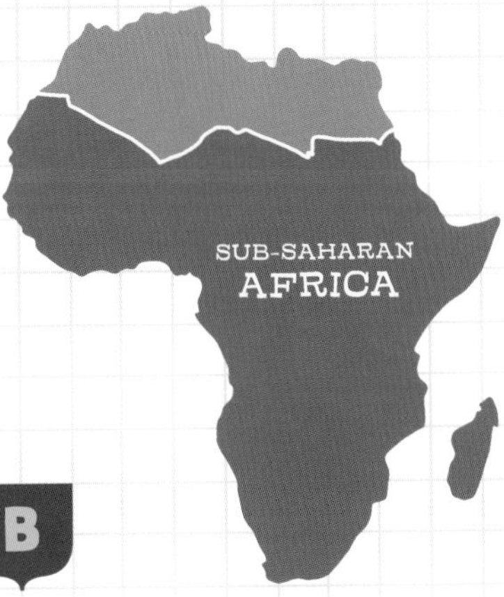
SUB-SAHARAN
AFRICA

B

C

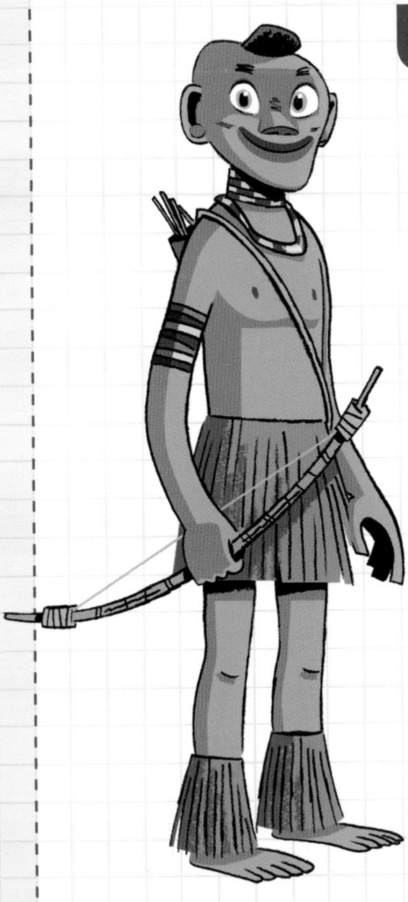

D

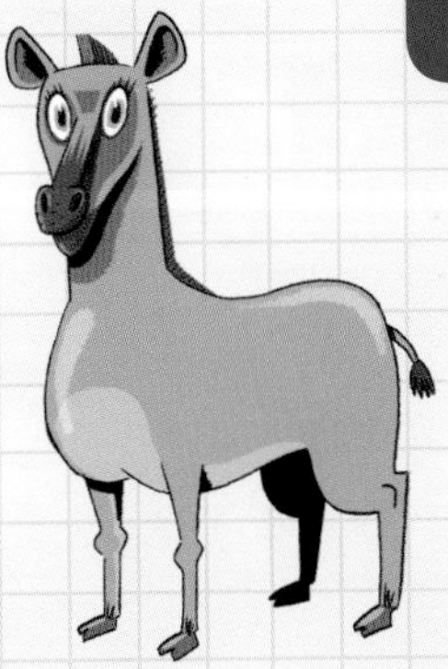

E

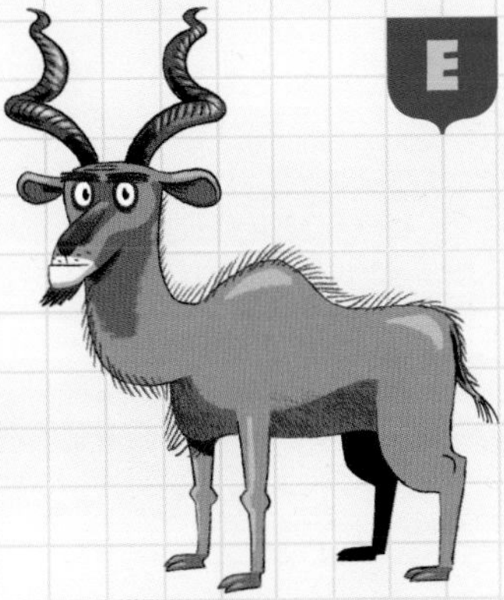

F

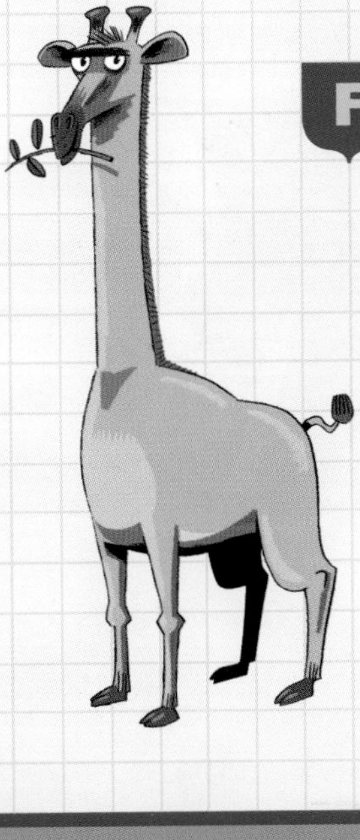

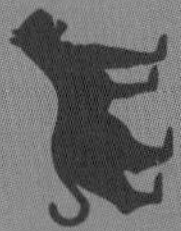

1

2

3

4

5

KIPLING'S OBSERVATION

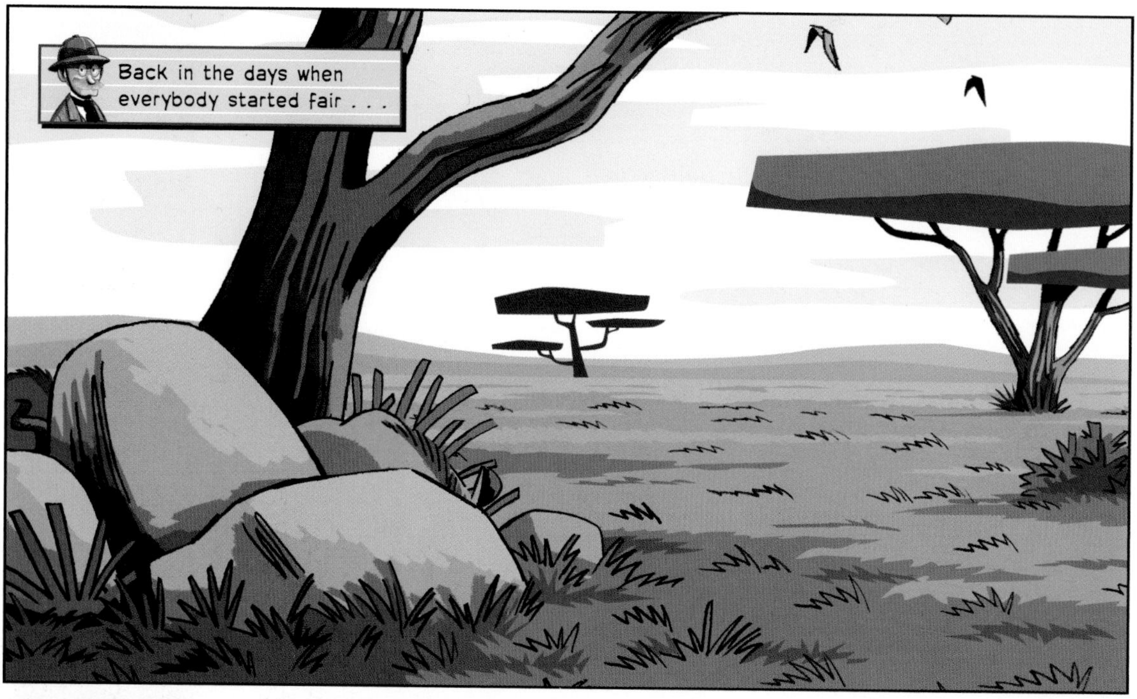
Back in the days when everybody started fair . . .

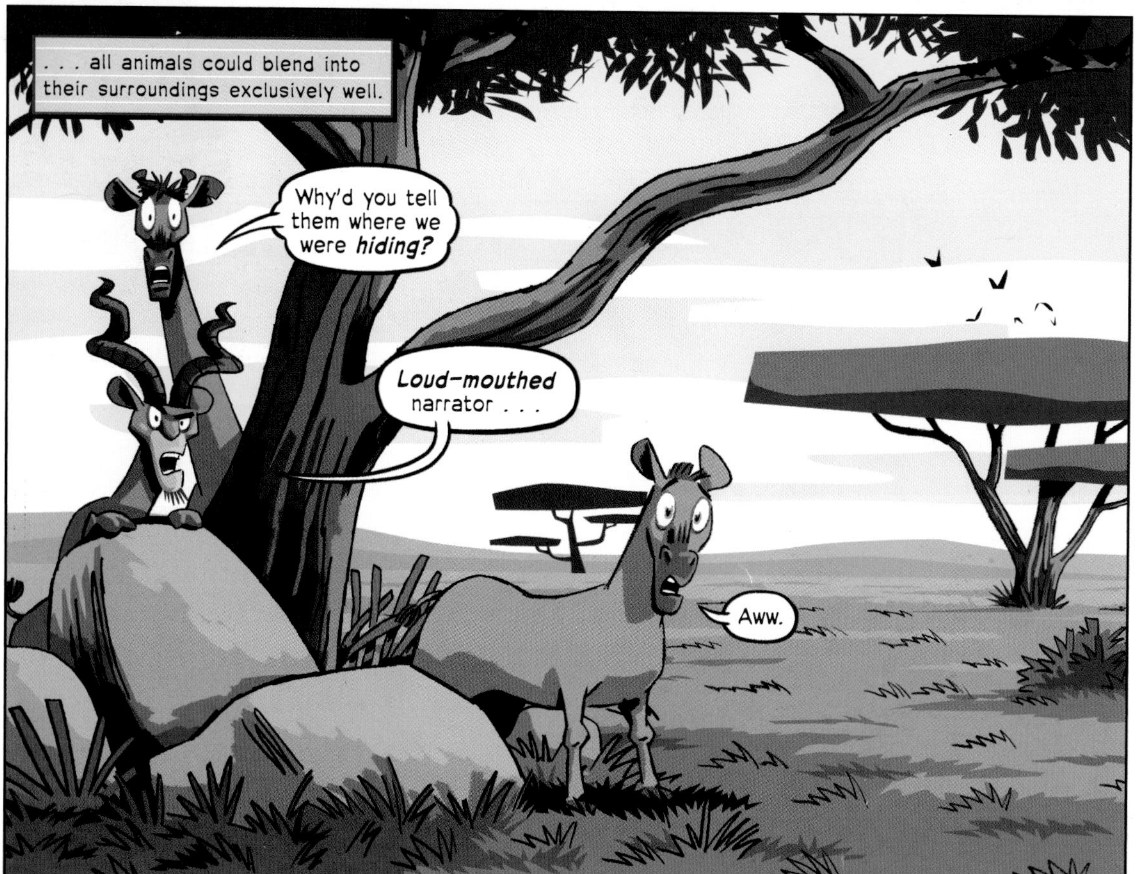
. . . all animals could blend into their surroundings exclusively well.
Why'd you tell them where we were *hiding?*
Loud-mouthed narrator . . .
Aww.

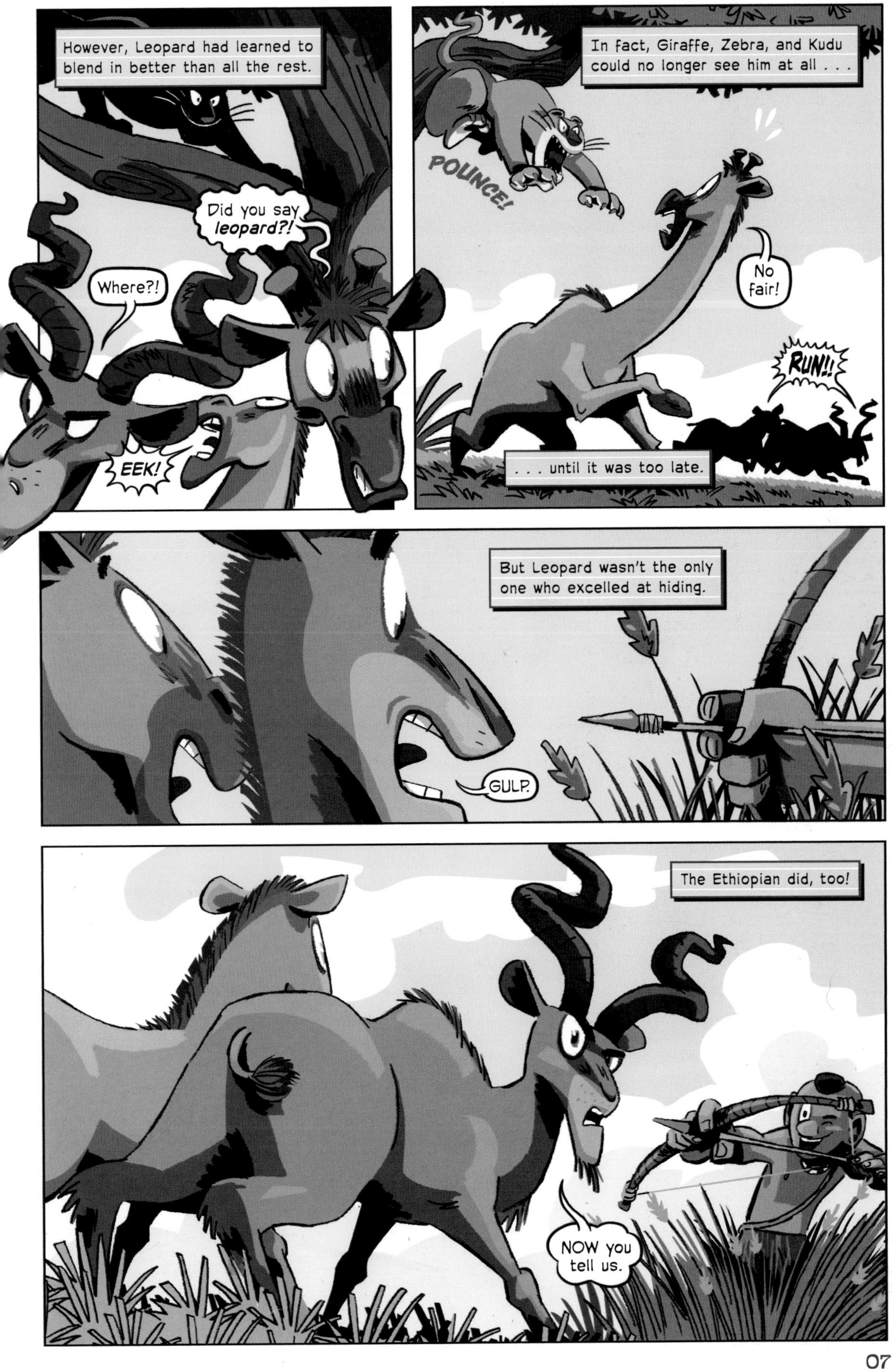
However, Leopard had learned to blend in better than all the rest.
Did you say leopard?!
Where?!
EEK!
In fact, Giraffe, Zebra, and Kudu could no longer see him at all . . .
POUNCE!
No fair!
RUN!!
. . . until it was too late.
But Leopard wasn't the only one who excelled at hiding.
GULP.
The Ethiopian did, too!
NOW you tell us.

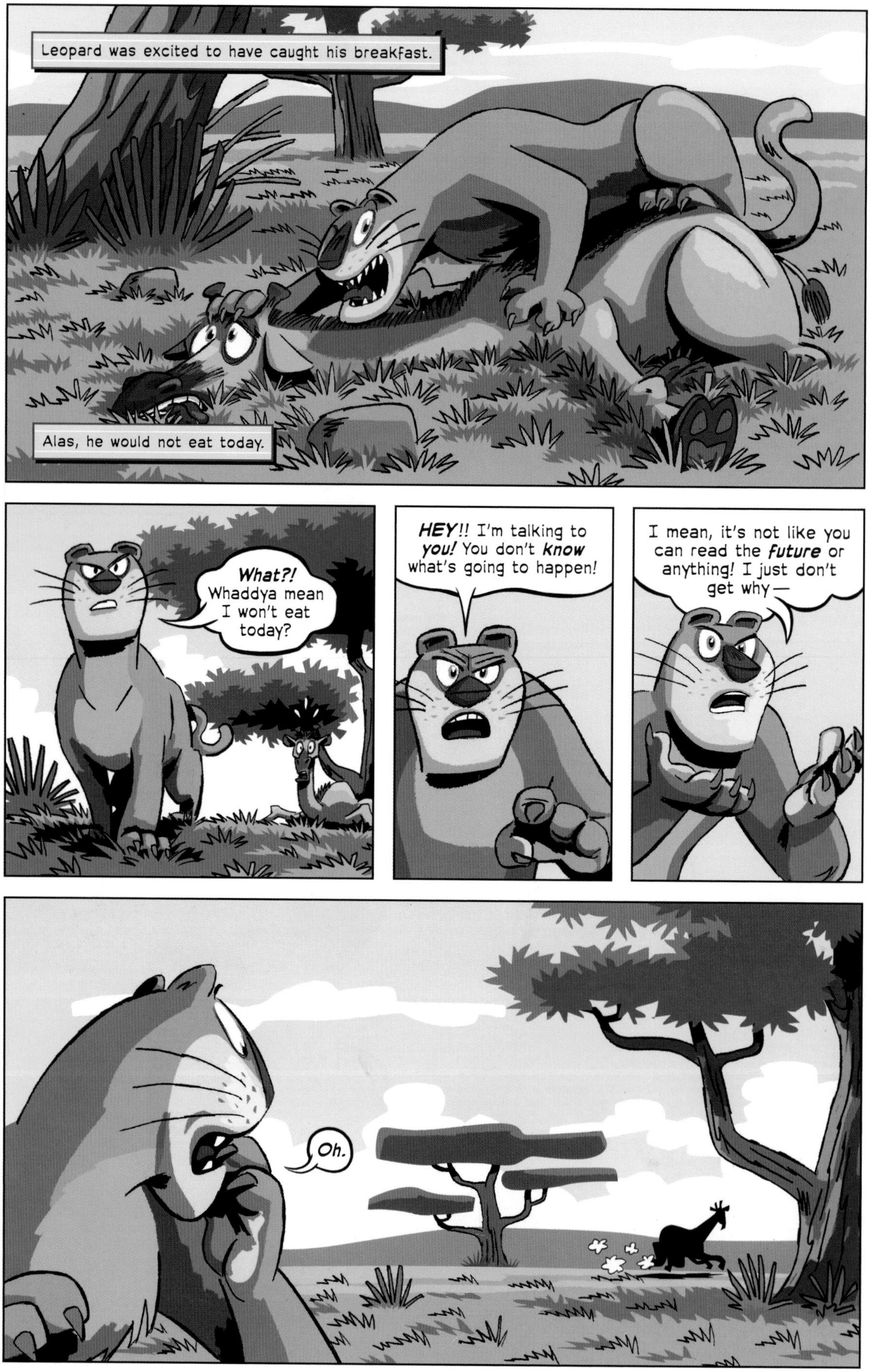
Leopard was excited to have caught his breakfast.
Alas, he would not eat today.
What?! Whaddya mean I won't eat today?
HEY!! I'm talking to you! You don't know what's going to happen!
I mean, it's not like you can read the future or anything! I just don't get why—
Oh.

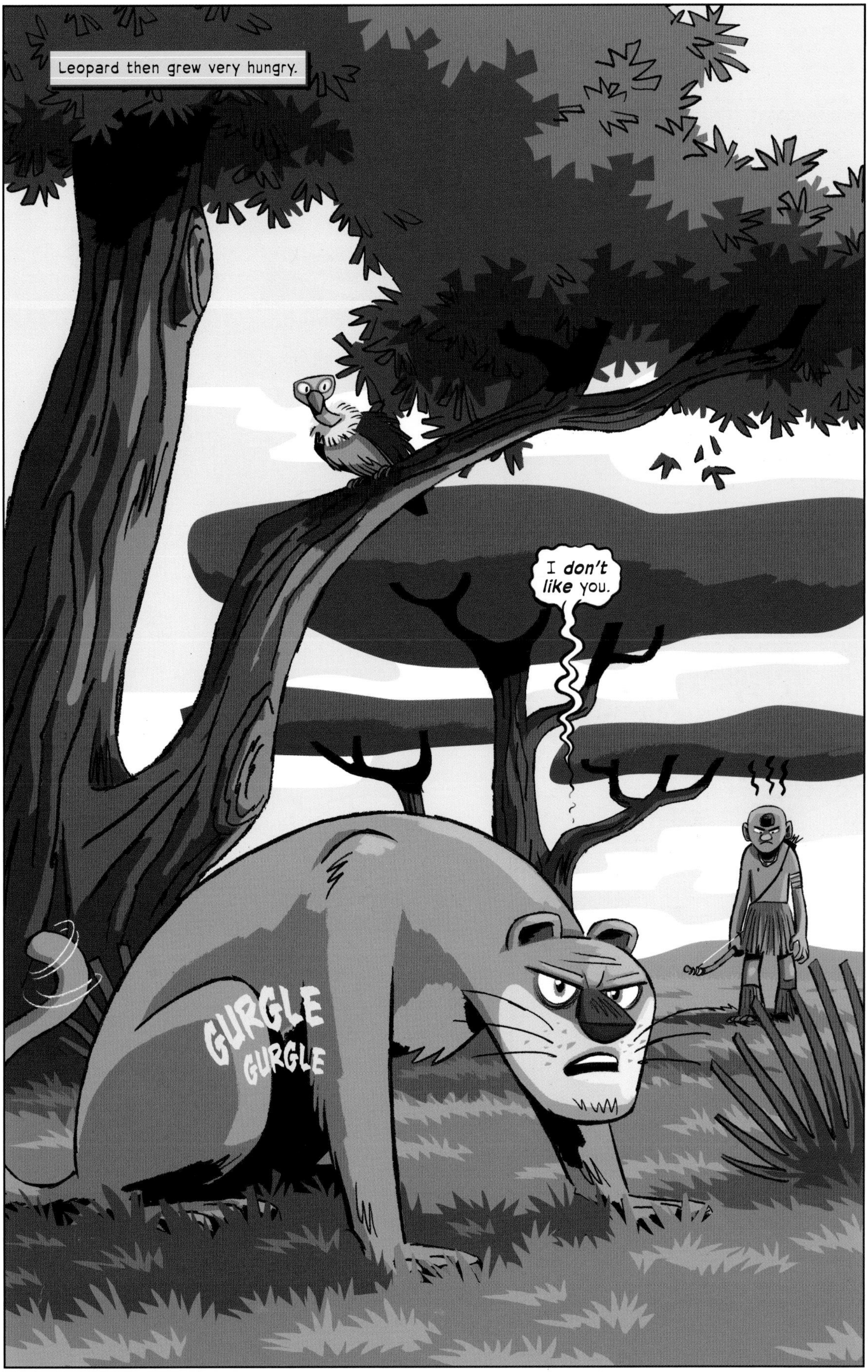
Leopard then grew very hungry.
I *don't* *like* you.
GURGLE
GURGLE

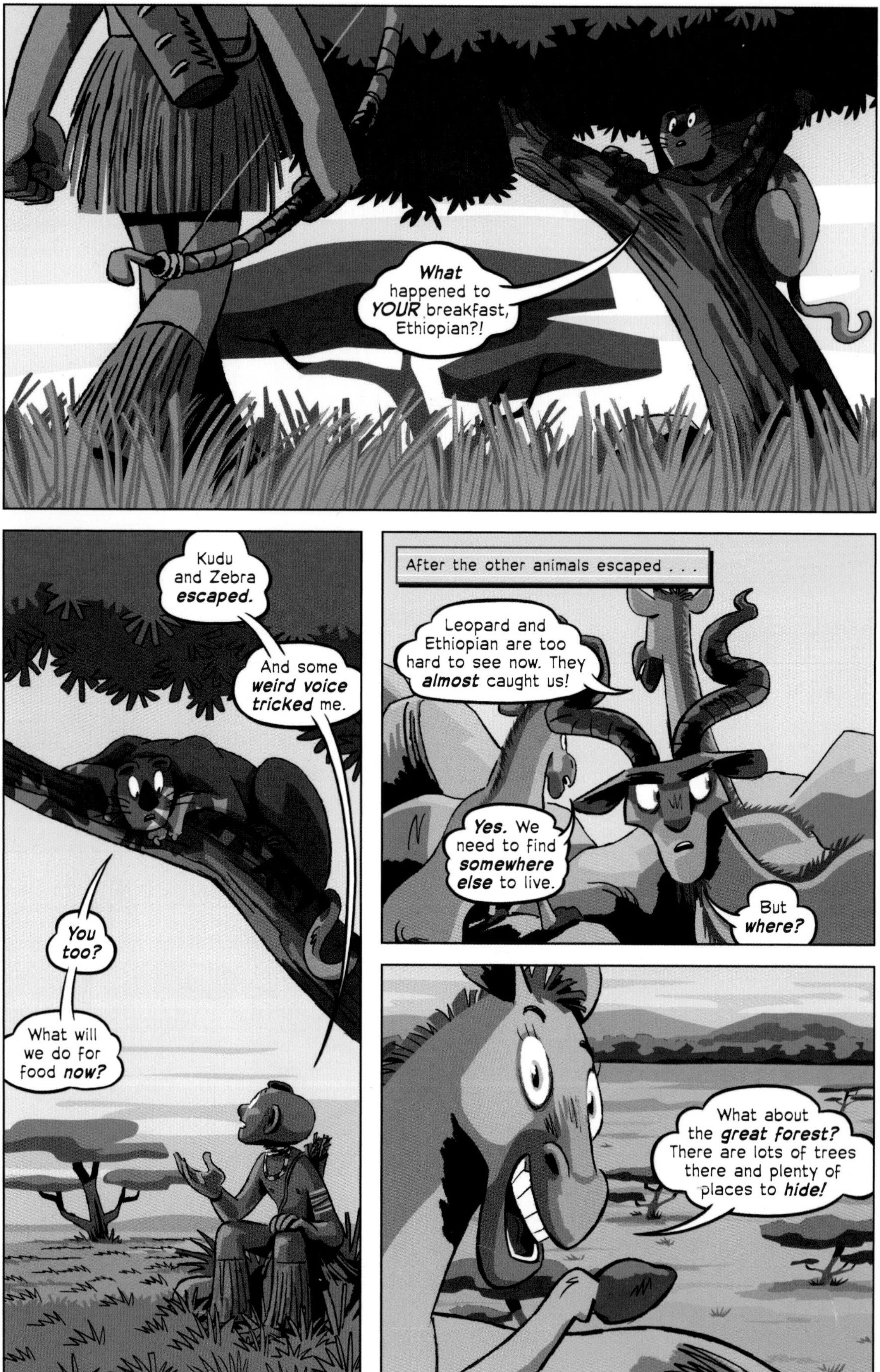

What happened to YOUR breakfast, Ethiopian?!
Kudu and Zebra escaped.
And some weird voice tricked me.
You too?
What will we do for food now?
After the other animals escaped . . .
Leopard and Ethiopian are too hard to see now. They almost caught us!
Yes. We need to find somewhere else to live.
But where?
What about the great forest? There are lots of trees there and plenty of places to hide!

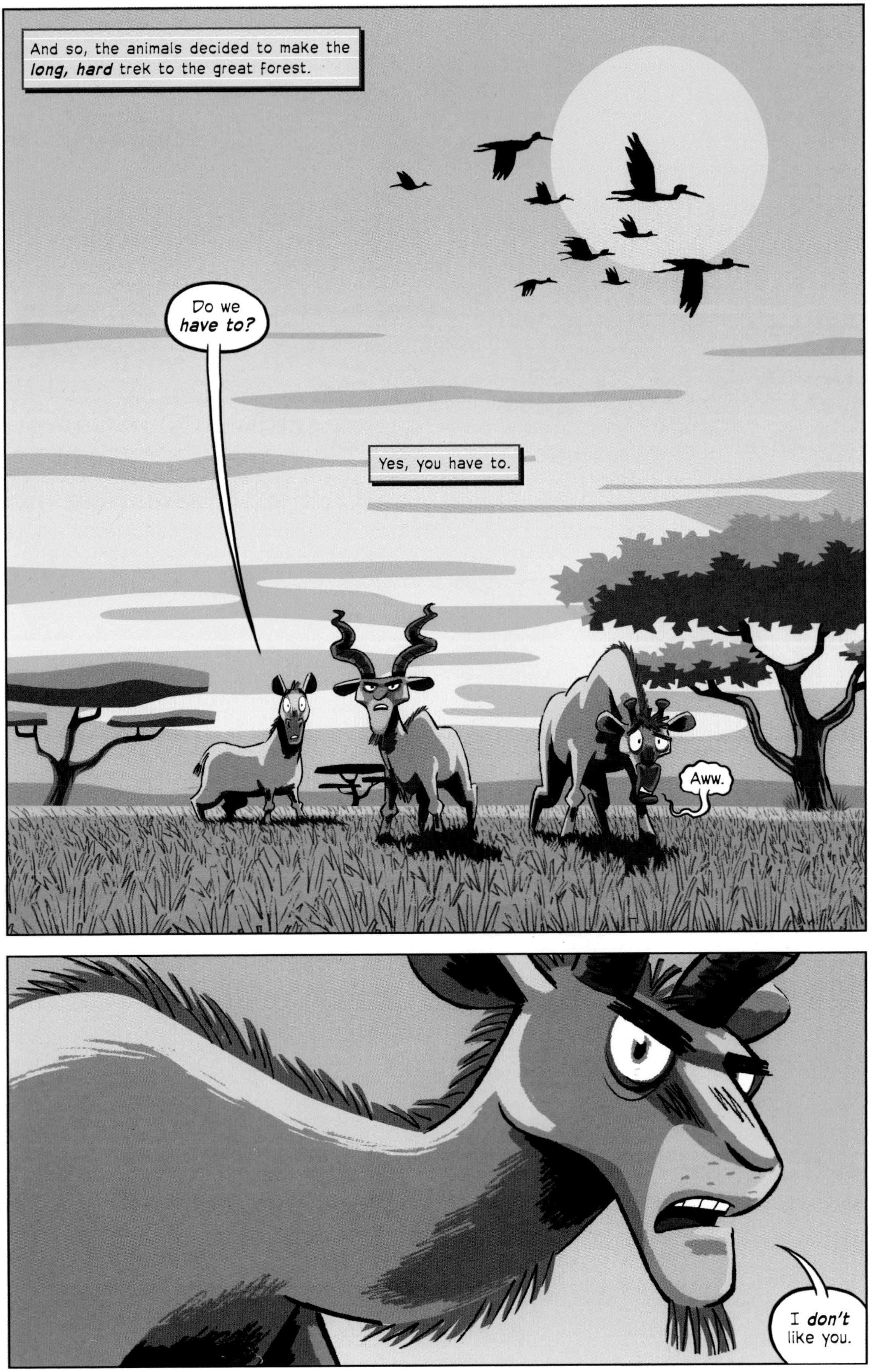
And so, the animals decided to make the *long, hard* trek to the great forest.
Do we *have to?*
Yes, you have to.
Aww.
I *don't* like you.

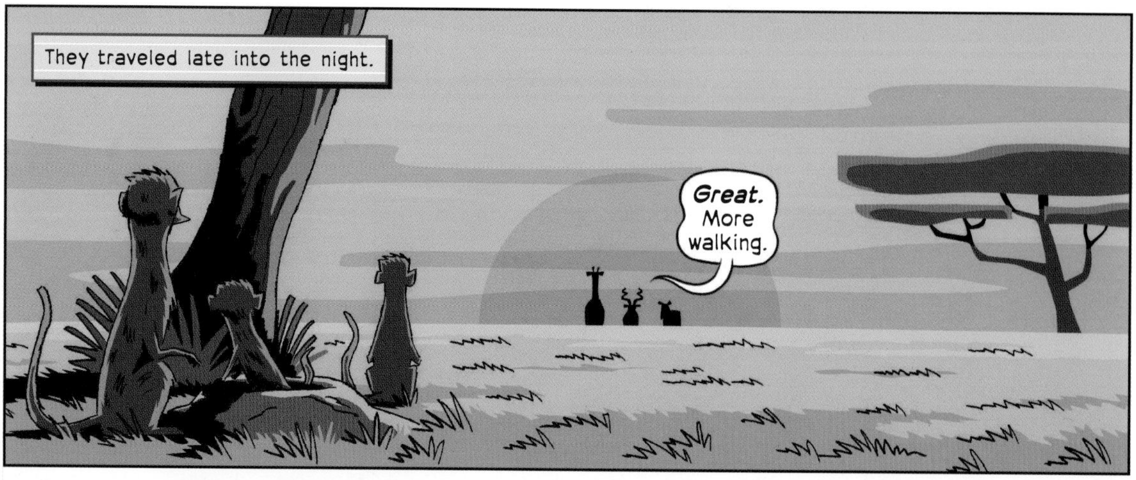
They traveled late into the night.
Great. More walking.

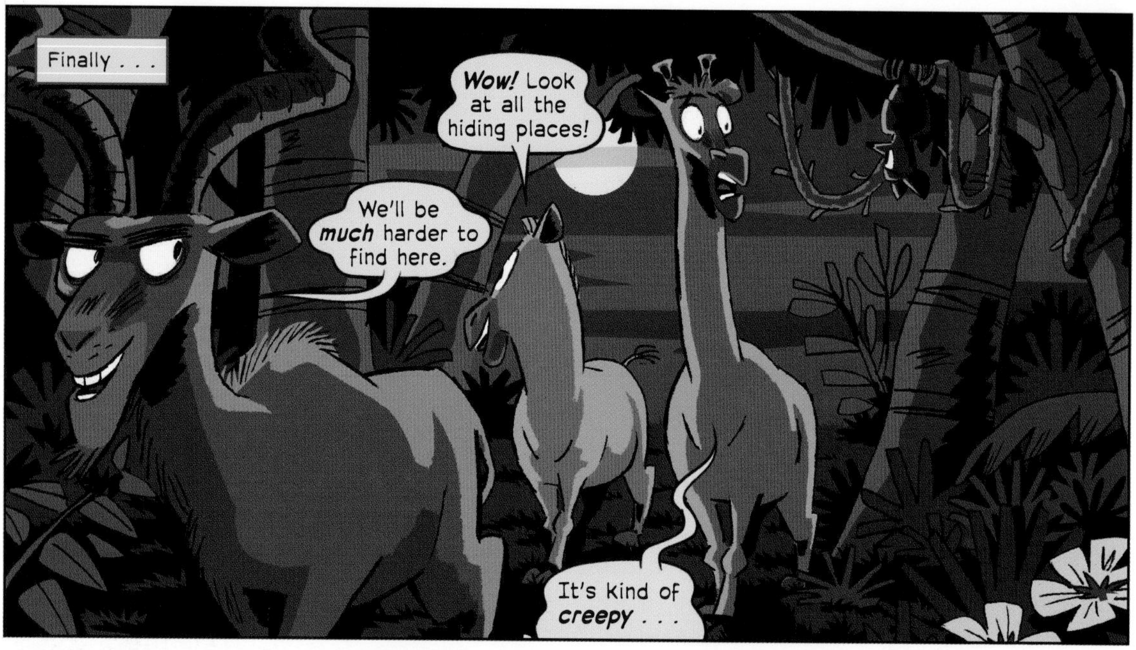
Finally . . .
Wow! Look at all the hiding places!
We'll be much harder to find here.
It's kind of creepy . . .

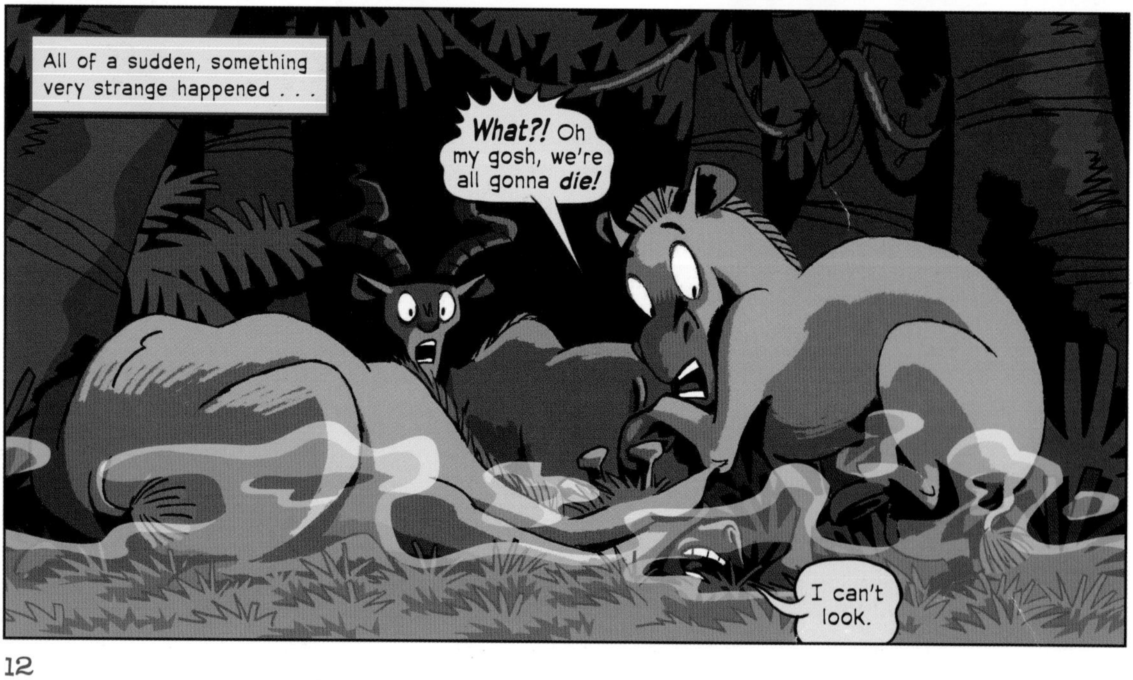
All of a sudden, something very strange happened . . .
What?! Oh my gosh, we're all gonna die!
I can't look.

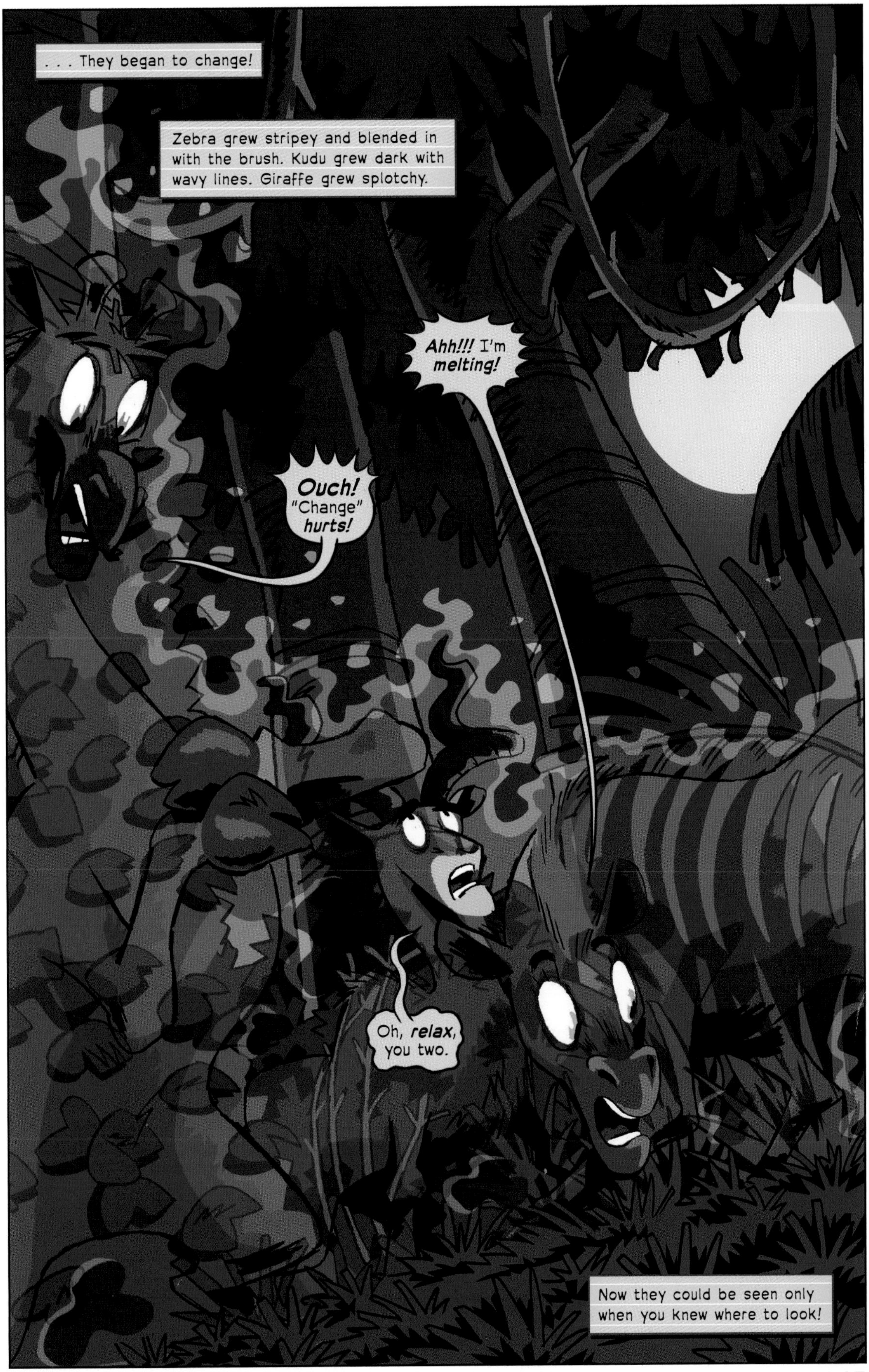
. . . They began to change!
Zebra grew stripey and blended in with the brush. Kudu grew dark with wavy lines. Giraffe grew splotchy.
Ahh!!! I'm melting!
Ouch! "Change" hurts!
Oh, relax, you two.
Now they could be seen only when you knew where to look!

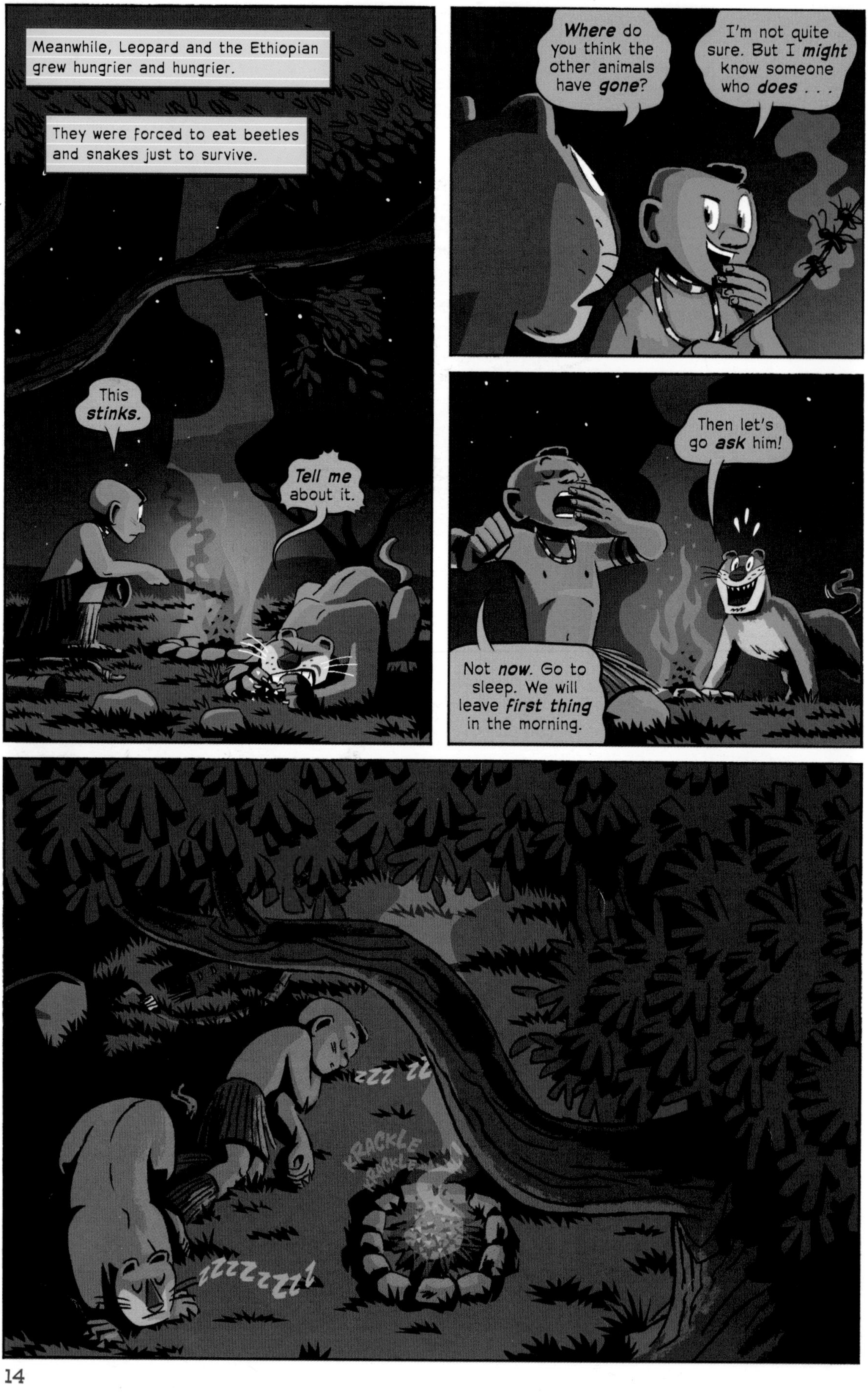
Meanwhile, Leopard and the Ethiopian grew hungrier and hungrier.
They were forced to eat beetles and snakes just to survive.
This **stinks.**
Tell me about it.
Where do you think the other animals have ***gone***?
I'm not quite sure. But I ***might*** know someone who ***does*** . . .
Then let's go ***ask*** him!
Not ***now***. Go to sleep. We will leave ***first thing*** in the morning.
KRACKLE
KRACKLE

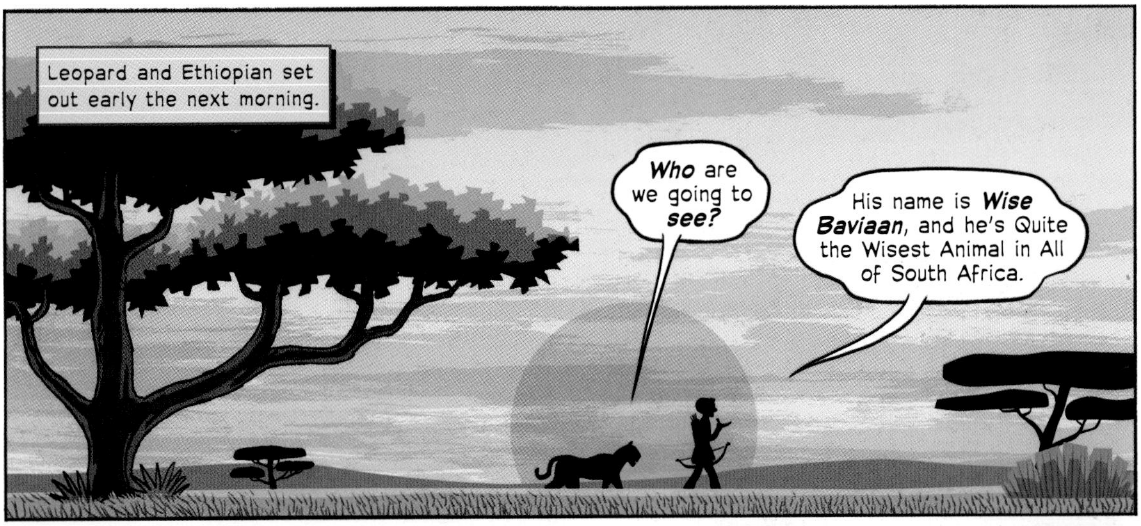
Leopard and Ethiopian set out early the next morning.
Who are we going to see?
His name is Wise Baviaan, and he's Quite the Wisest Animal in All of South Africa.

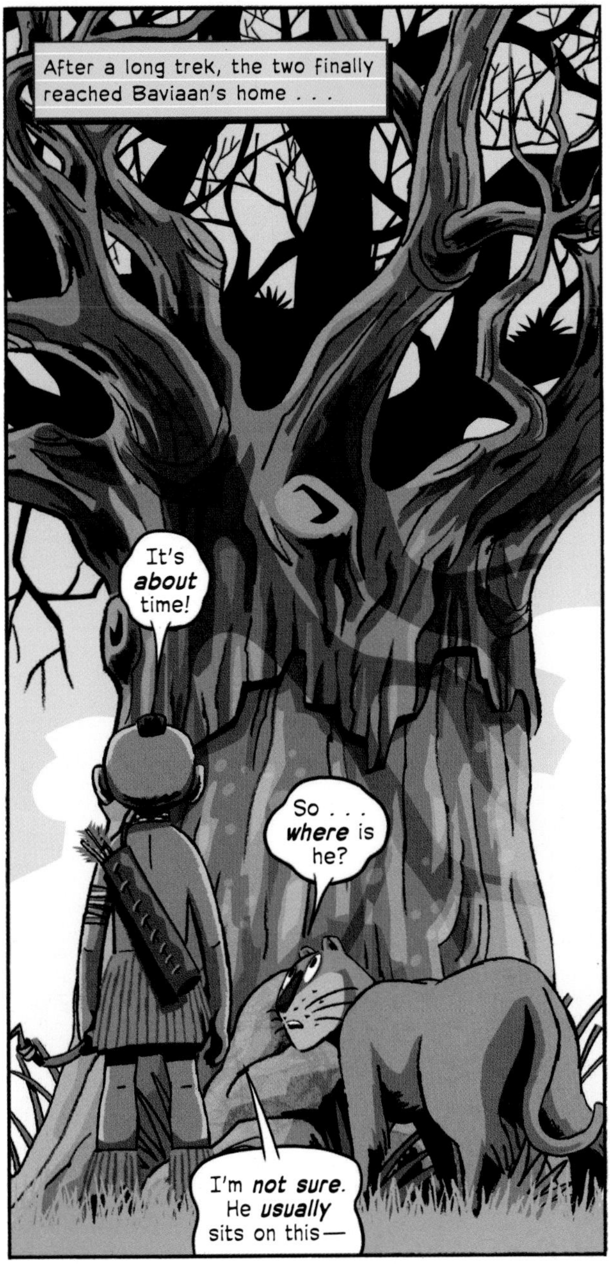
After a long trek, the two finally reached Baviaan's home . . .
It's about time!
So . . . where is he?
I'm not sure. He usually sits on this—

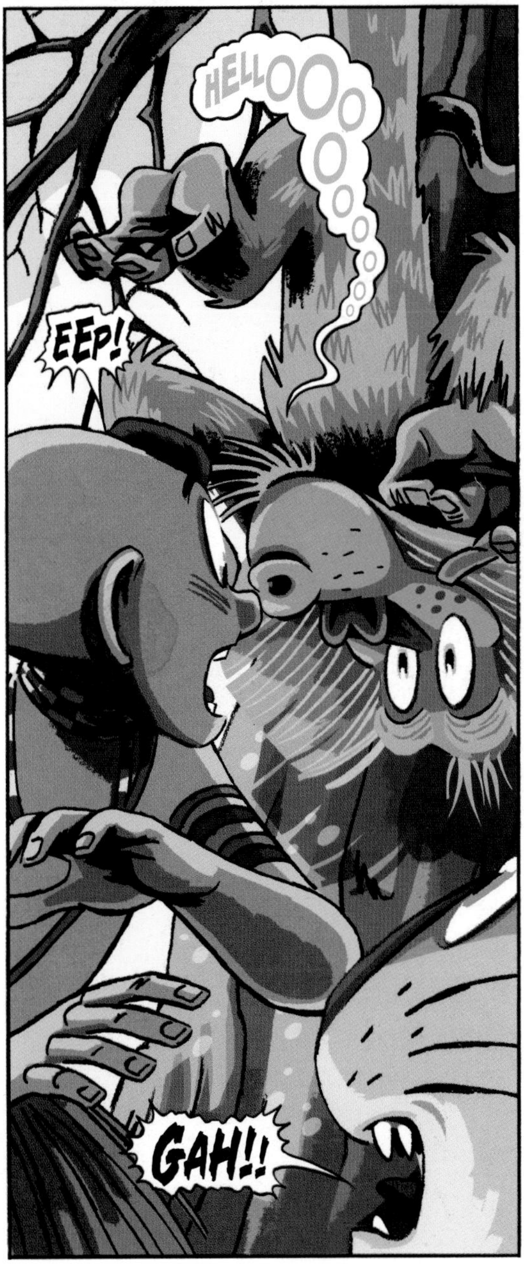
HELLOOOOOOOOO
EEP!
GAH!!

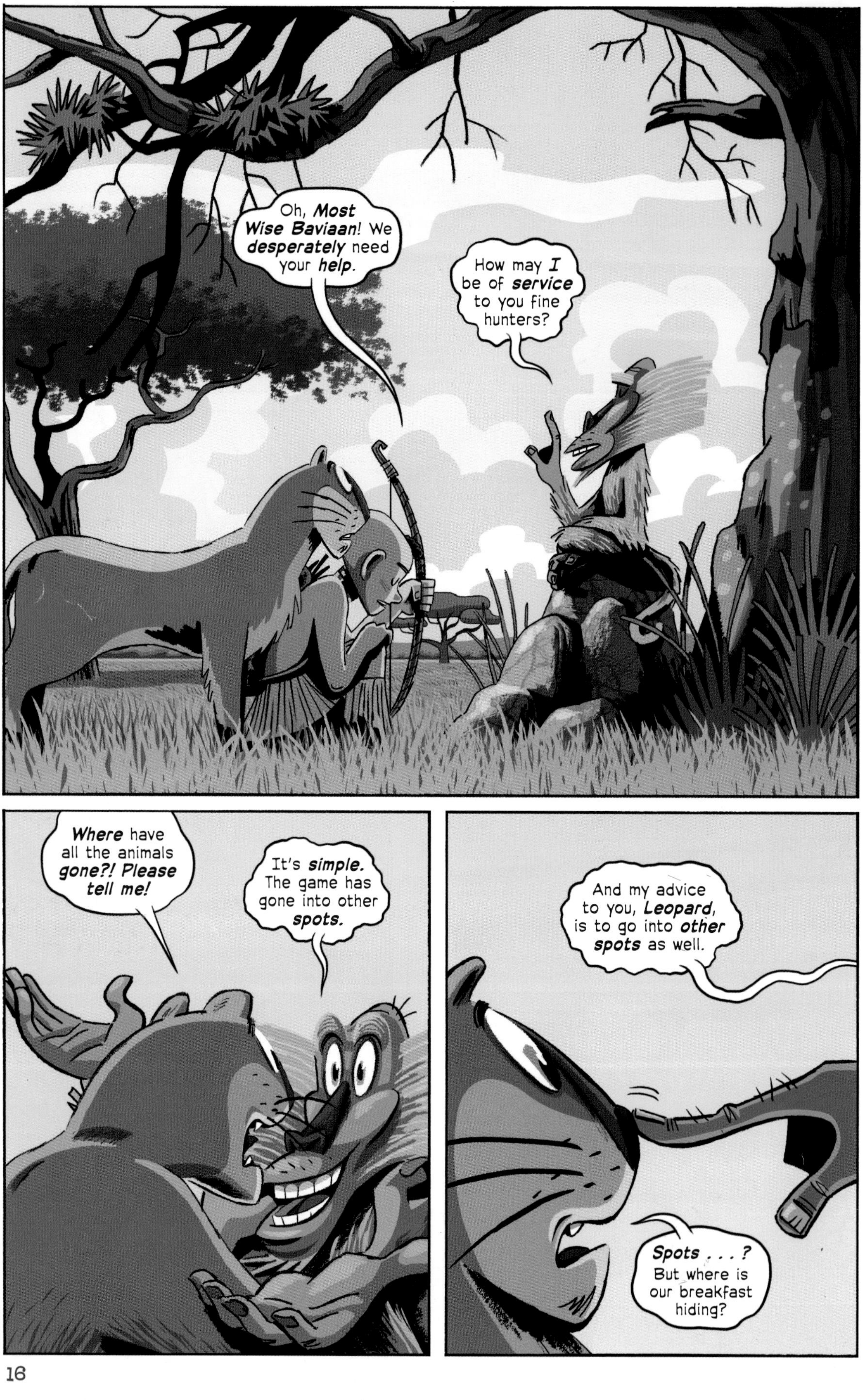
Oh, **Most Wise Baviaan**! We **desperately** need your **help**.
How may ***I*** be of **service** to you fine hunters?
Where have all the animals ***gone?! Please tell me!***
It's ***simple.*** The game has gone into other ***spots.***
And my advice to you, ***Leopard***, is to go into ***other spots*** as well.
Spots . . . ? But where is our breakfast hiding?

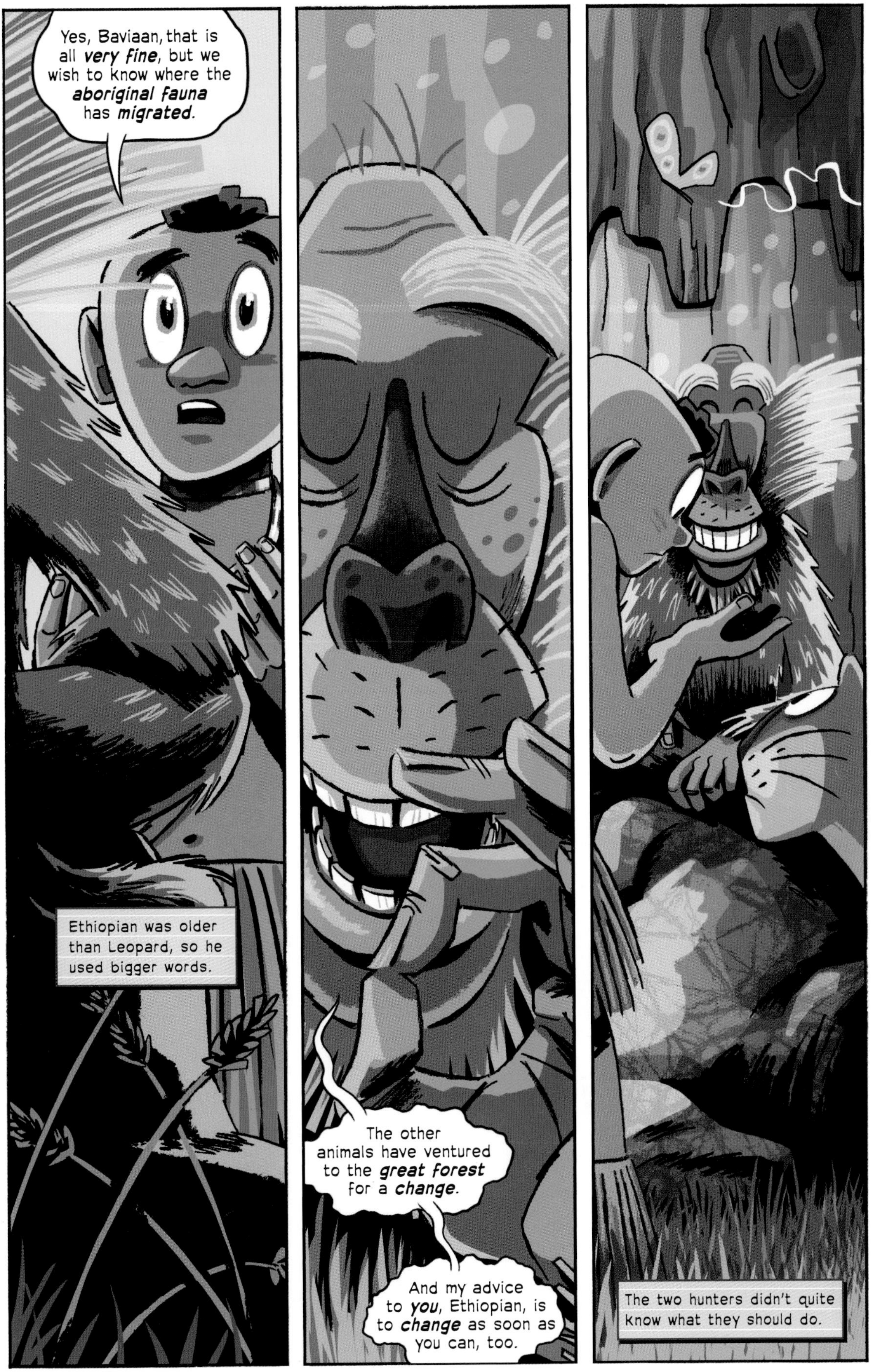
Yes, Baviaan, that is all *very fine*, but we wish to know where the *aboriginal fauna* has *migrated.*
Ethiopian was older than Leopard, so he used bigger words.
The other animals have ventured to the *great forest* for a *change*.
And my advice to *you*, Ethiopian, is to *change* as soon as you can, too.
The two hunters didn't quite know what they should do.

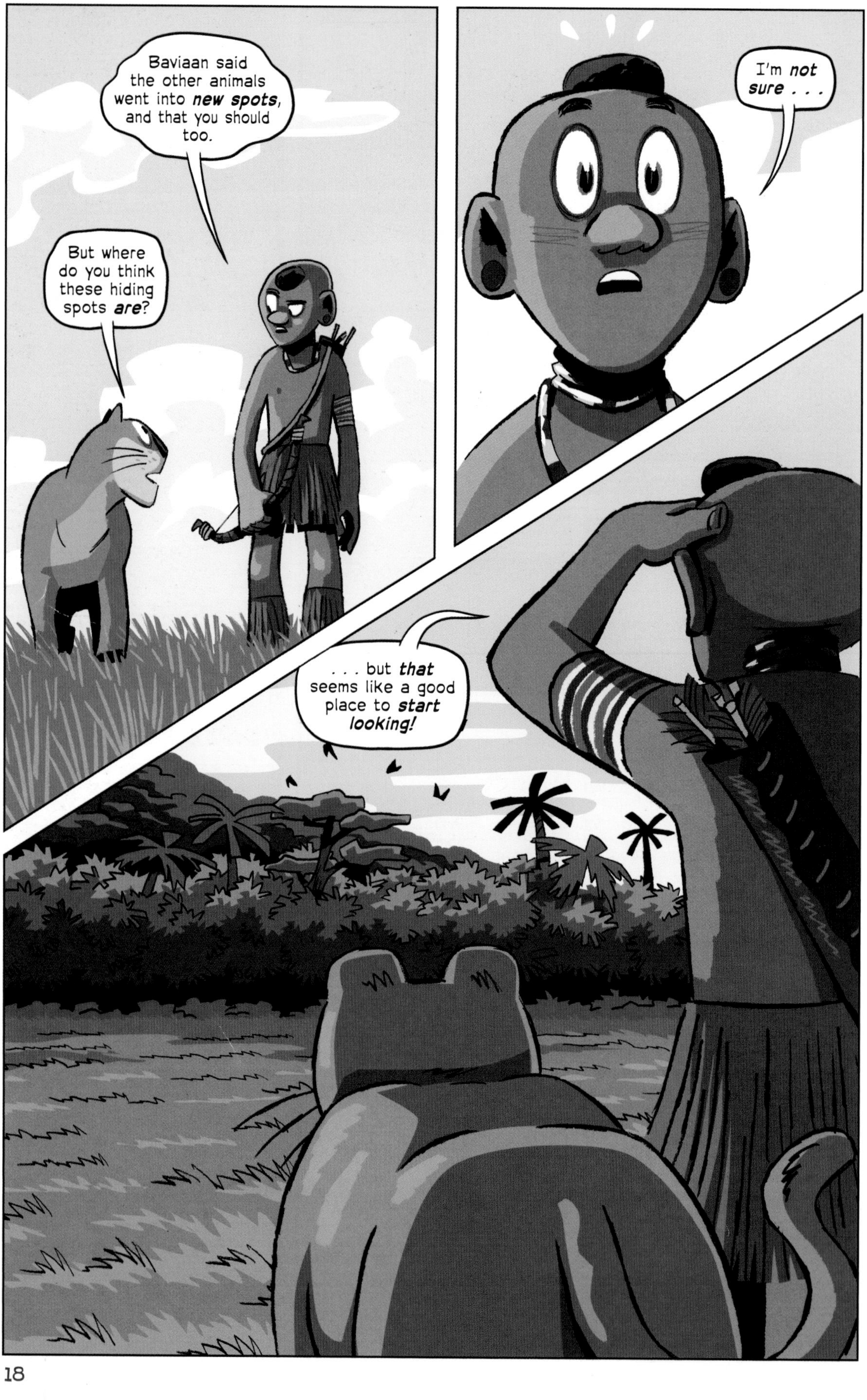
Baviaan said the other animals went into ***new spots***, and that you should too.
But where do you think these hiding spots ***are***?
I'm ***not sure . . .***
. . . but ***that*** seems like a good place to ***start looking!***

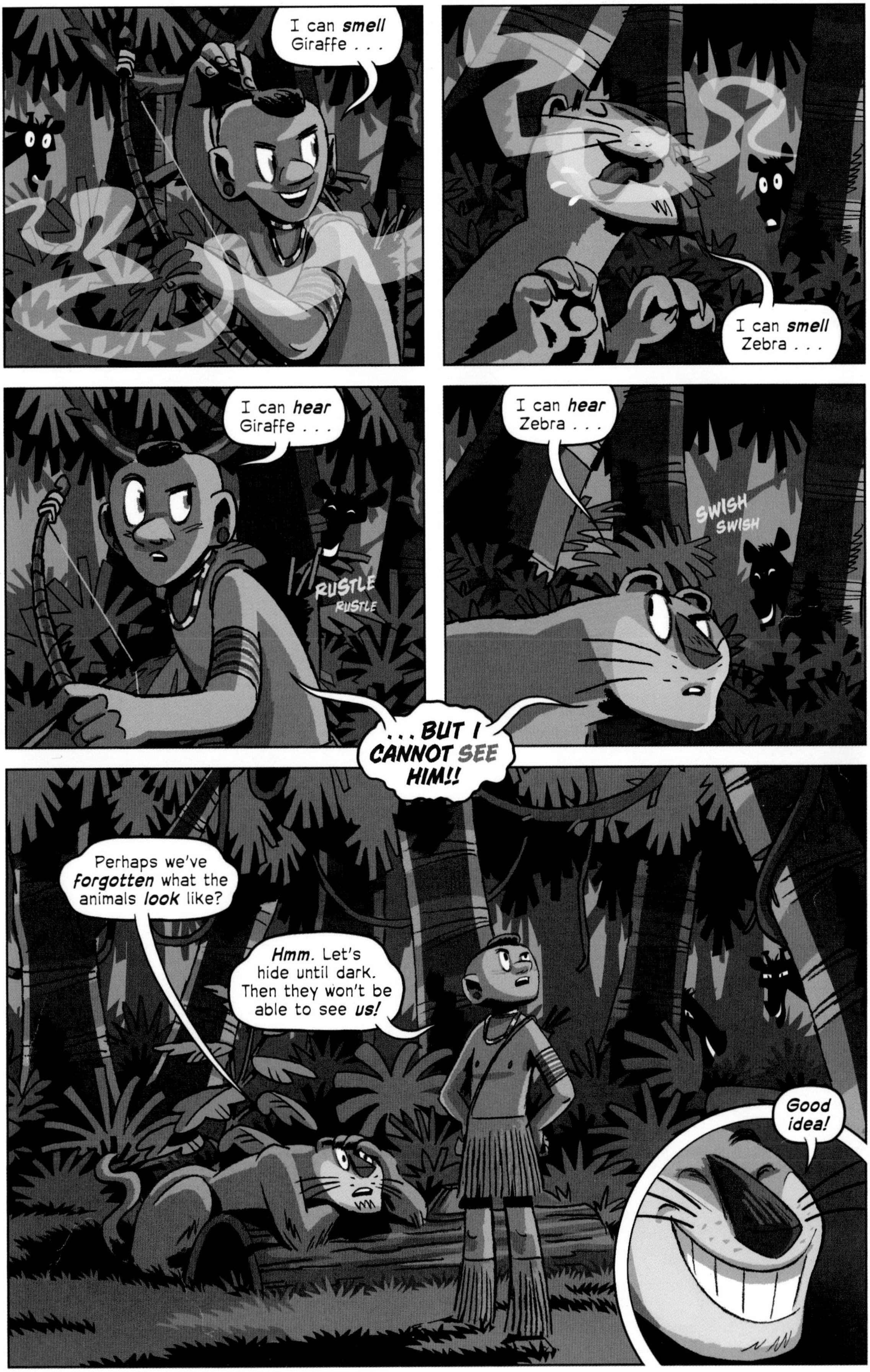

I can *smell* Giraffe . . .
I can *smell* Zebra . . .
I can *hear* Giraffe . . .
RUSTLE
RUSTLE
I can *hear* Zebra . . .
SWISH
SWISH
. . . BUT I CANNOT SEE HIM!!
Perhaps we've *forgotten* what the animals *look* like?
Hmm. Let's hide until dark. Then they won't be able to see *us!*
Good idea!

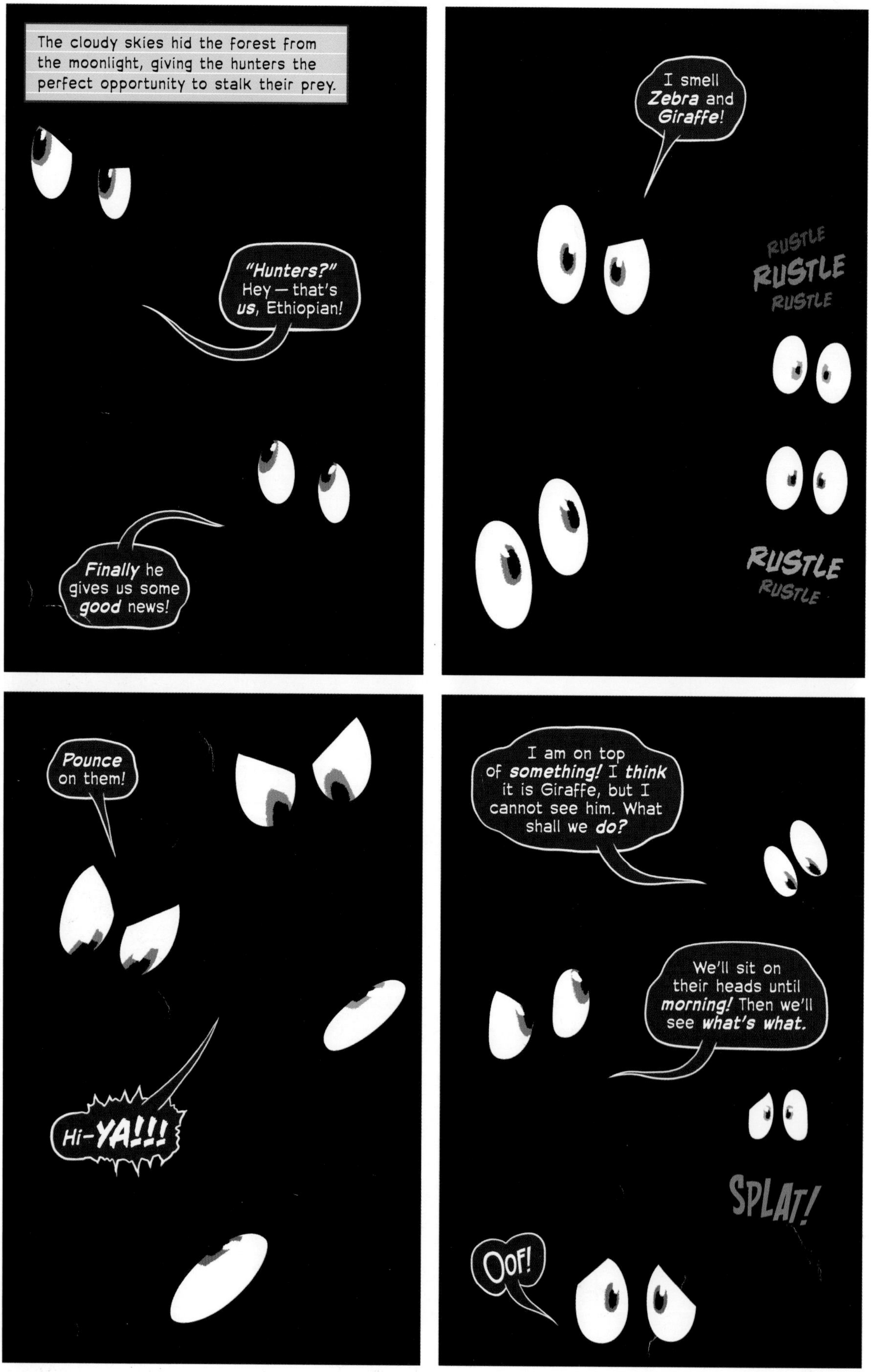

The cloudy skies hid the forest from the moonlight, giving the hunters the perfect opportunity to stalk their prey.
"Hunters?" Hey — that's us, Ethiopian!
Finally he gives us some good news!
I smell Zebra and Giraffe!
RUSTLE RUSTLE RUSTLE
RUSTLE RUSTLE
Pounce on them!
Hi-YA!!!
I am on top of something! I think it is Giraffe, but I cannot see him. What shall we do?
We'll sit on their heads until morning! Then we'll see what's what.
SPLAT!
OOF!

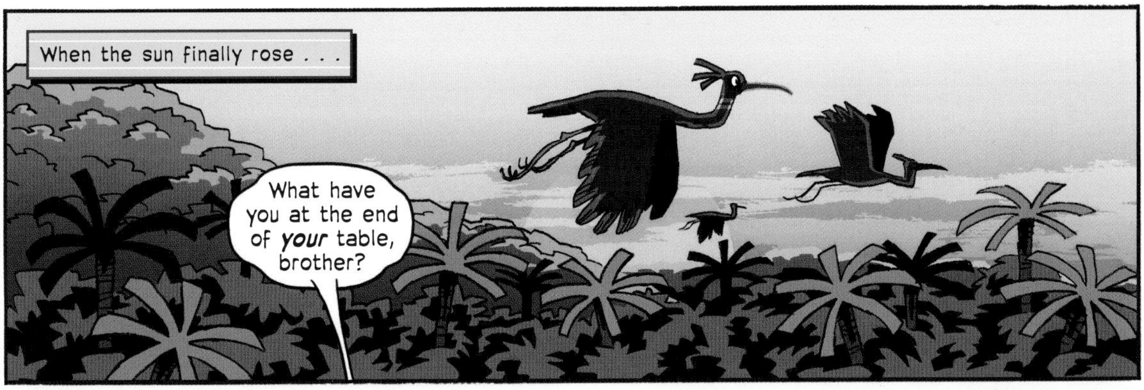
When the sun finally rose . . .
What have you at the end of *your* table, brother?

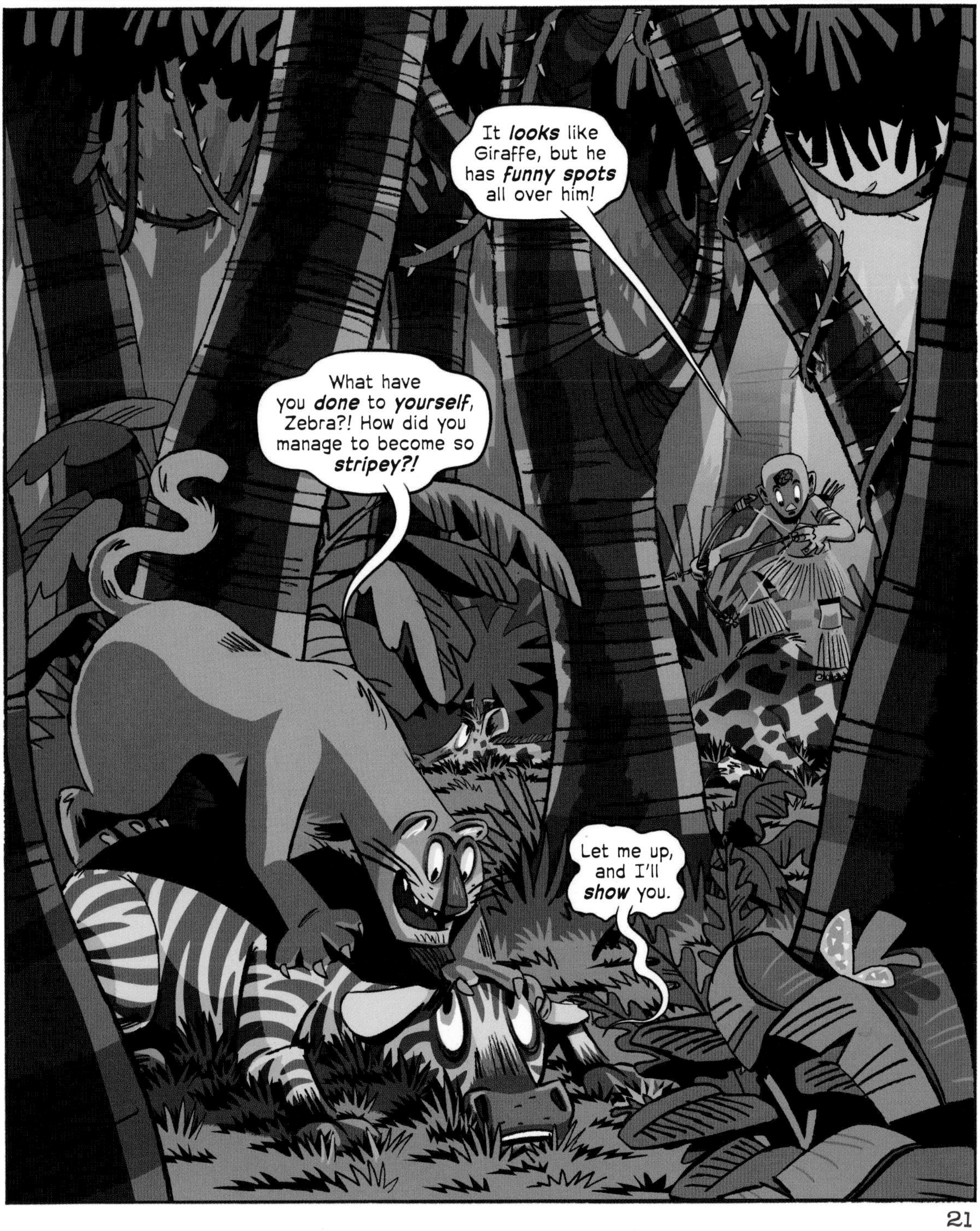
It *looks* like Giraffe, but he has *funny spots* all over him!
What have you *done* to *yourself*, Zebra?! How did you manage to become so *stripey?!*
Let me up, and I'll *show* you.

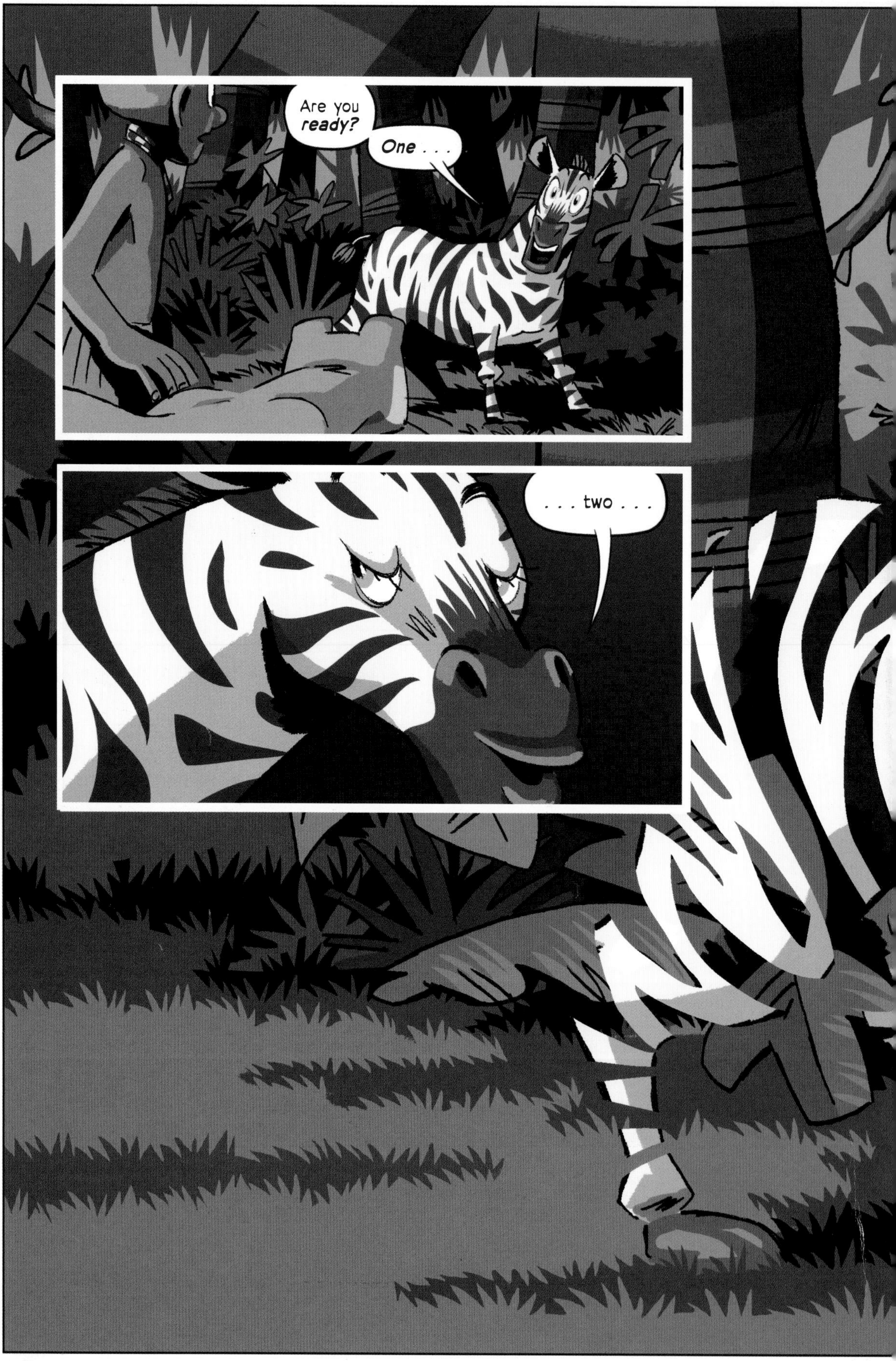
Are you ready?
One . . .
. . . two . . .

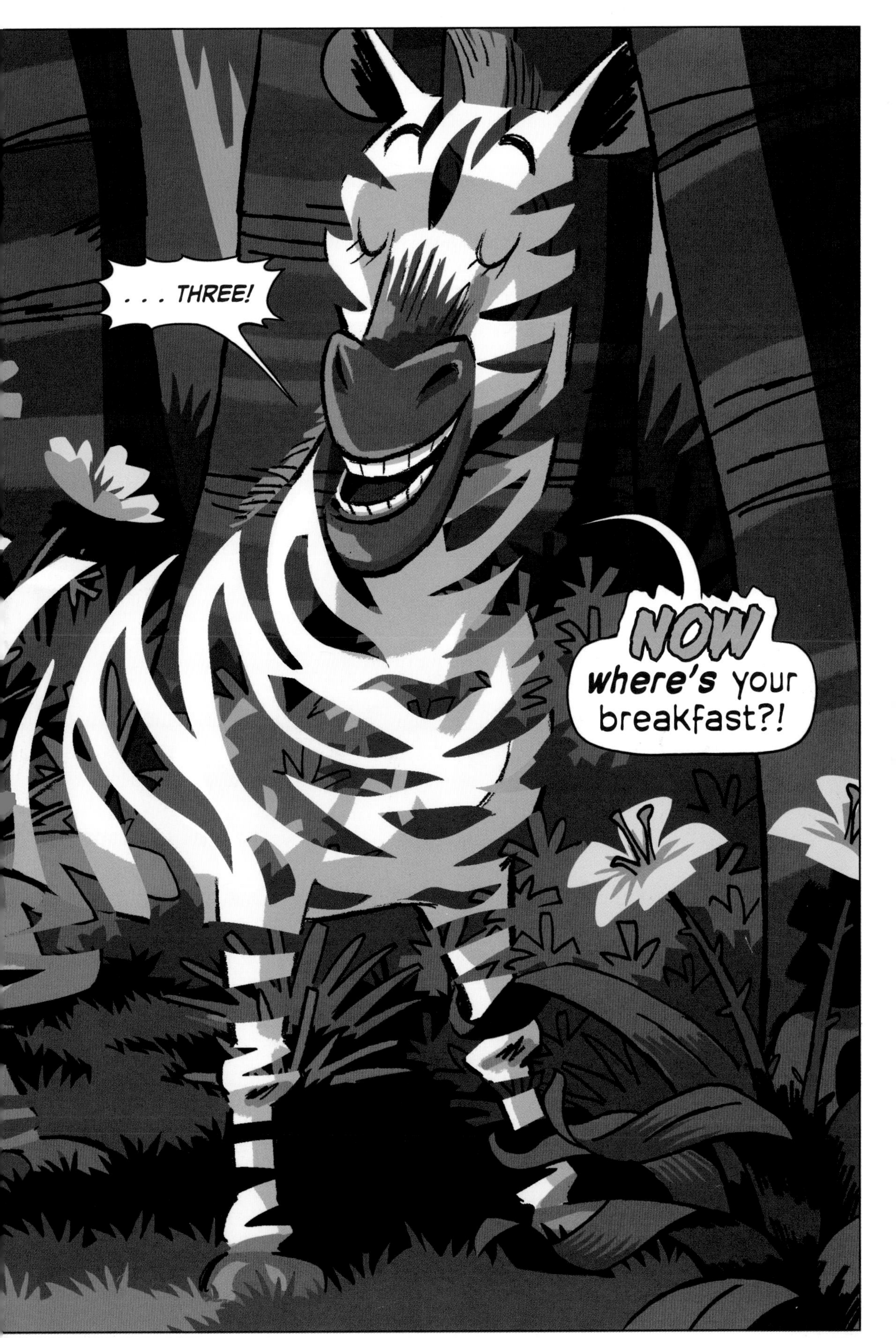
. . . THREE!
NOW where's your breakfast?!

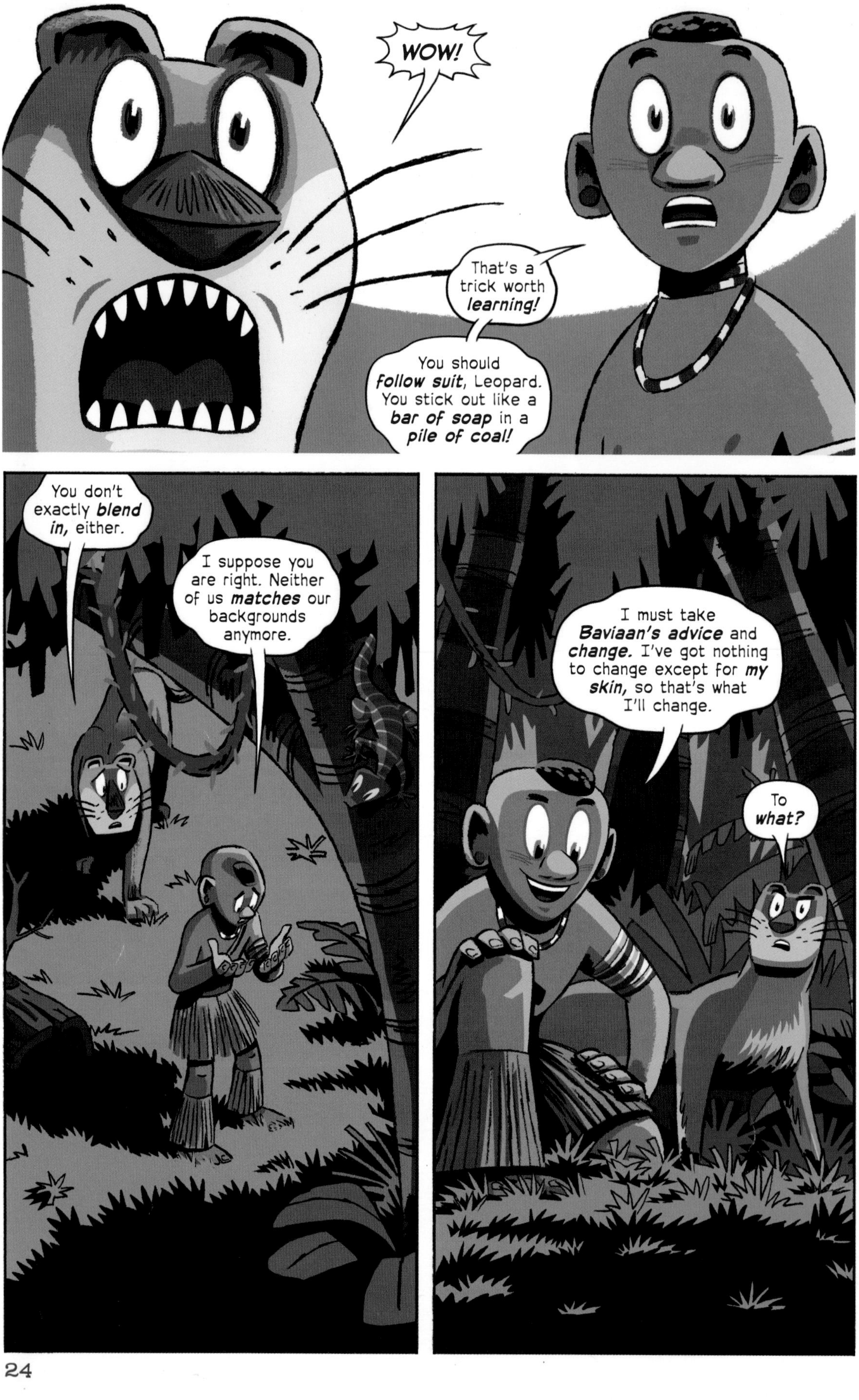
WOW!
That's a trick worth *learning!*
You should *follow suit*, Leopard. You stick out like a *bar of soap* in a *pile of coal!*
You don't exactly *blend in,* either.
I suppose you are right. Neither of us *matches* our backgrounds anymore.
I must take *Baviaan's advice* and *change.* I've got nothing to change except for *my skin,* so that's what I'll change.
To *what?*

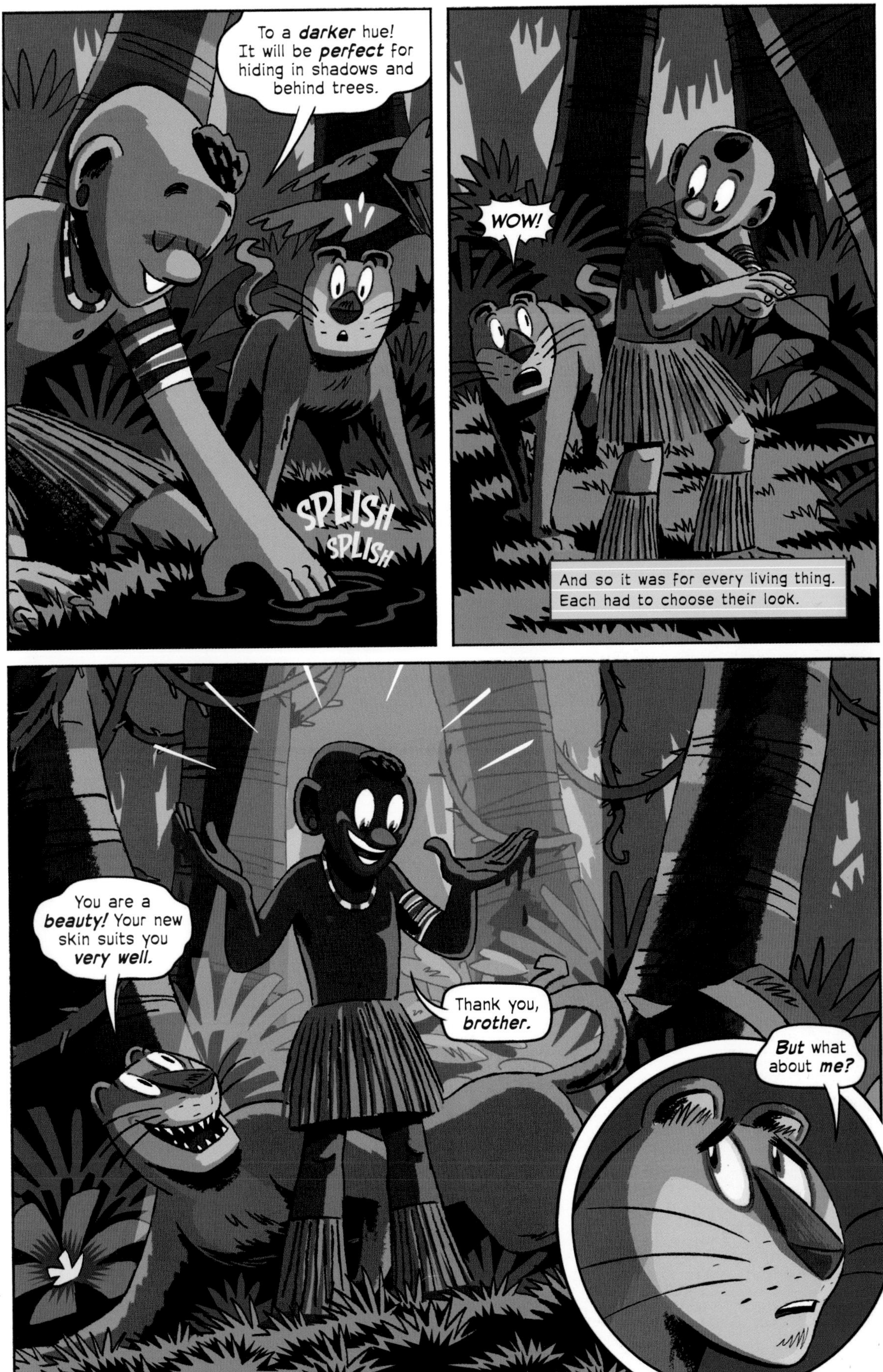
To a darker hue! It will be perfect for hiding in shadows and behind trees.
SPLISH
SPLISH
WOW!
And so it was for every living thing. Each had to choose their look.
You are a beauty! Your new skin suits you very well.
Thank you, brother.
But what about me?

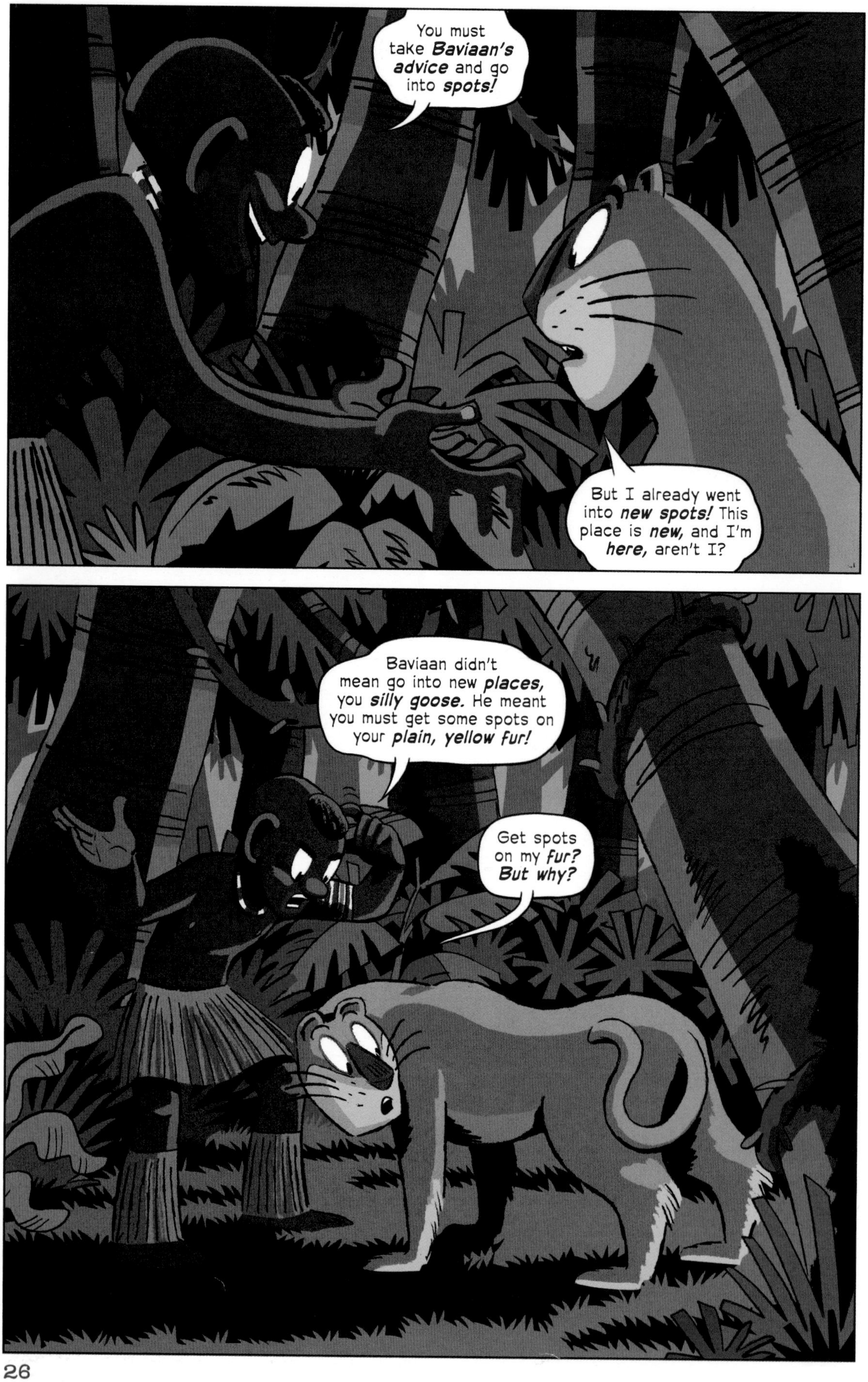
You must take Baviaan's advice and go into spots!
But I already went into new spots! This place is new, and I'm here, aren't I?
Baviaan didn't mean go into new places, you silly goose. He meant you must get some spots on your plain, yellow fur!
Get spots on my fur? But why?

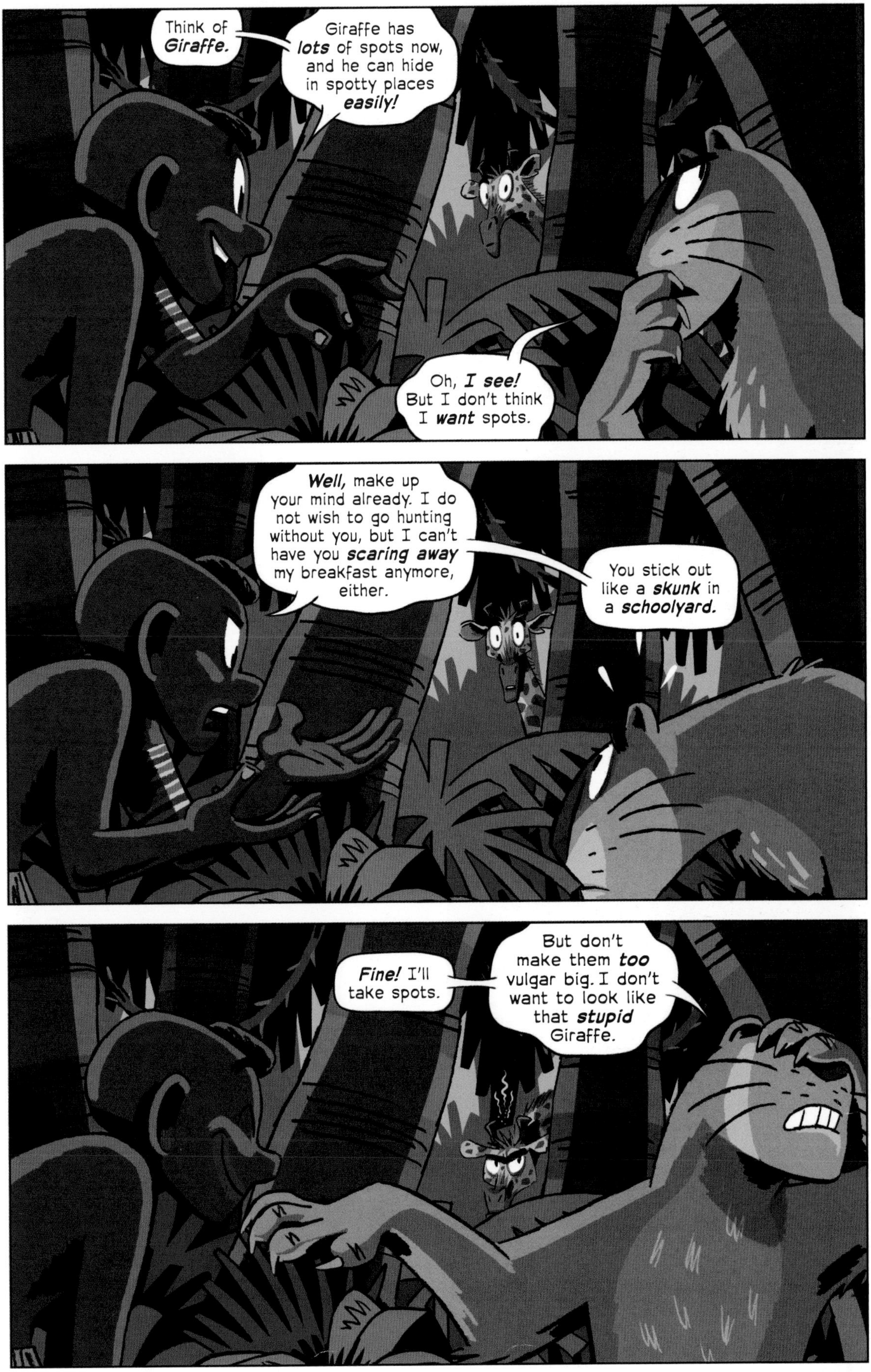
Think of *Giraffe.*
Giraffe has *lots* of spots now, and he can hide in spotty places *easily!*
Oh, *I see!* But I don't think I *want* spots.
Well, make up your mind already. I do not wish to go hunting without you, but I can't have you *scaring away* my breakfast anymore, either.
You stick out like a *skunk* in a *schoolyard.*
Fine! I'll take spots.
But don't make them *too* vulgar big. I don't want to look like that *stupid* Giraffe.

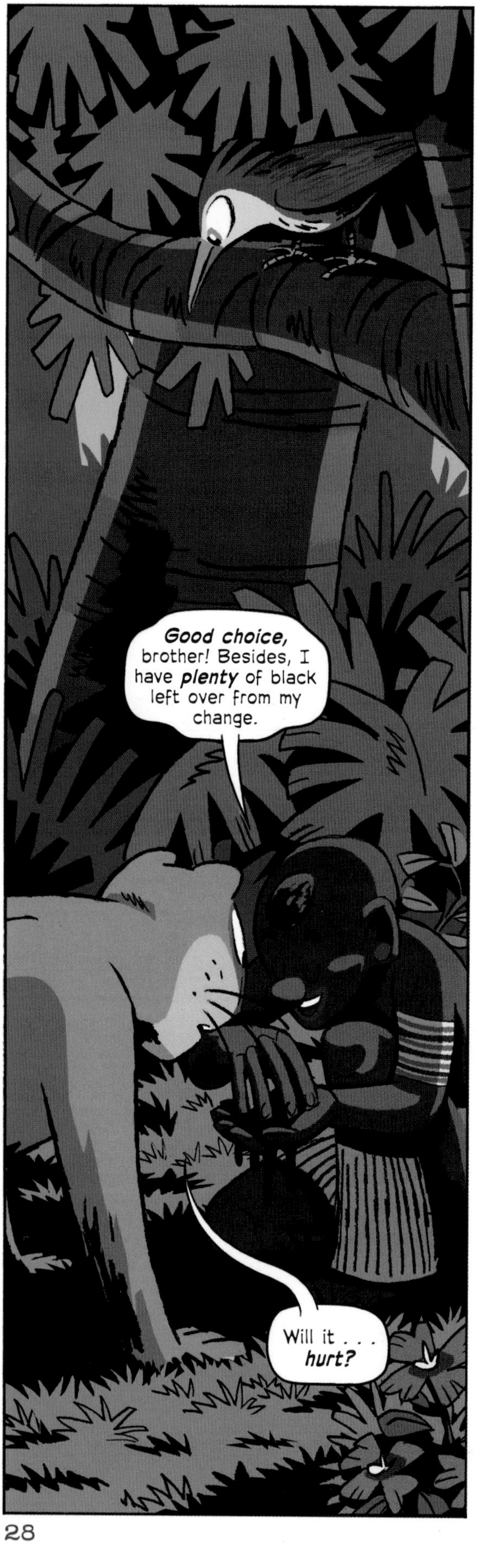
Good choice, brother! Besides, I have *plenty* of black left over from my change.
Will it . . . *hurt?*

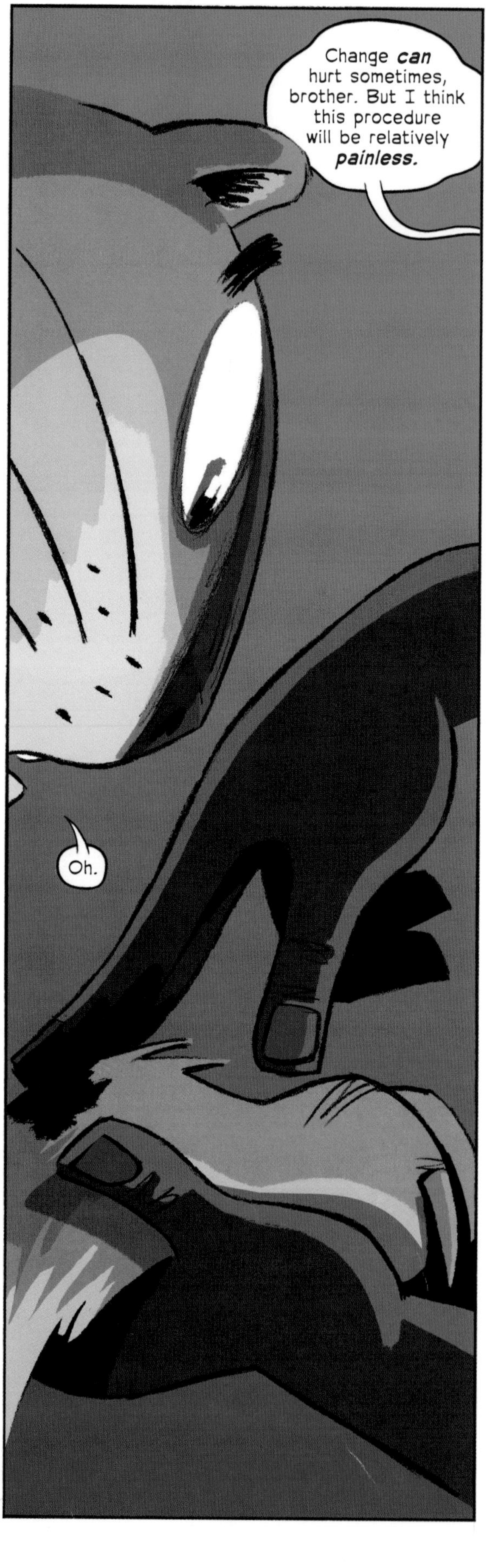
Change *can* hurt sometimes, brother. But I think this procedure will be relatively *painless.*
Oh.

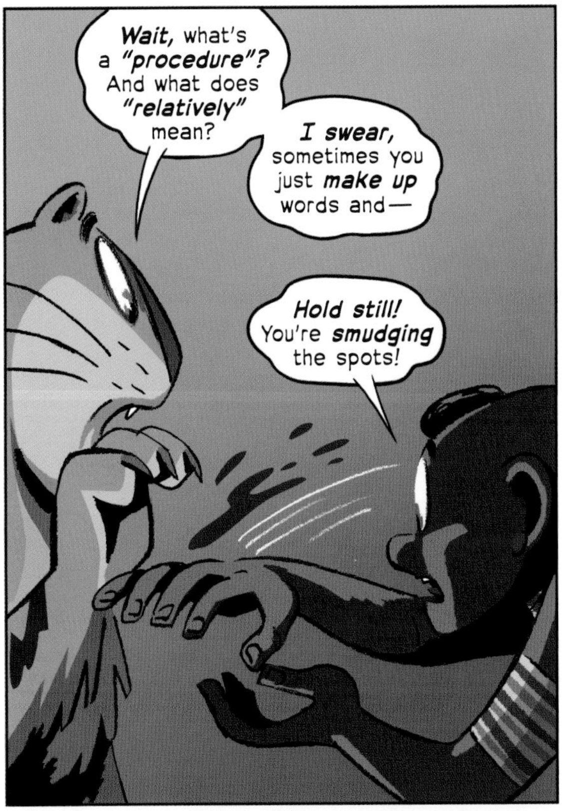
Wait, what's a "procedure"? And what does "relatively" mean?
I swear, sometimes you just make up words and—
Hold still! You're smudging the spots!

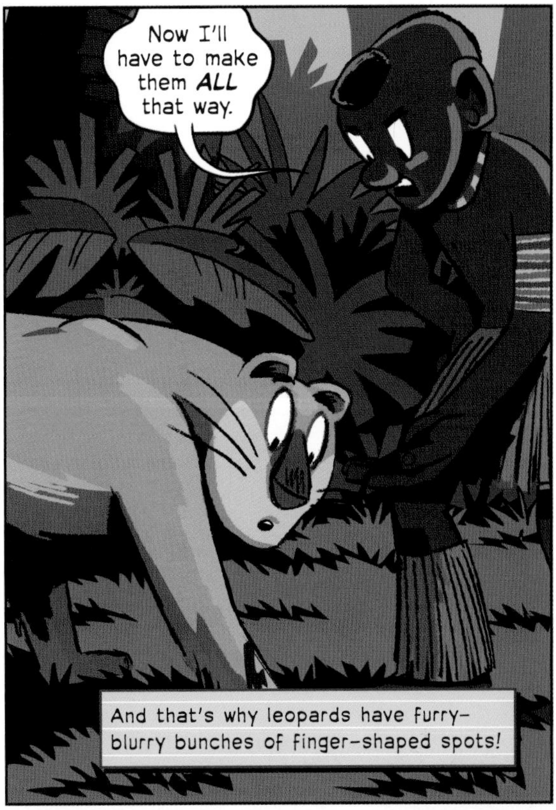
Now I'll have to make them ALL that way.
And that's why leopards have furry-blurry bunches of finger-shaped spots!

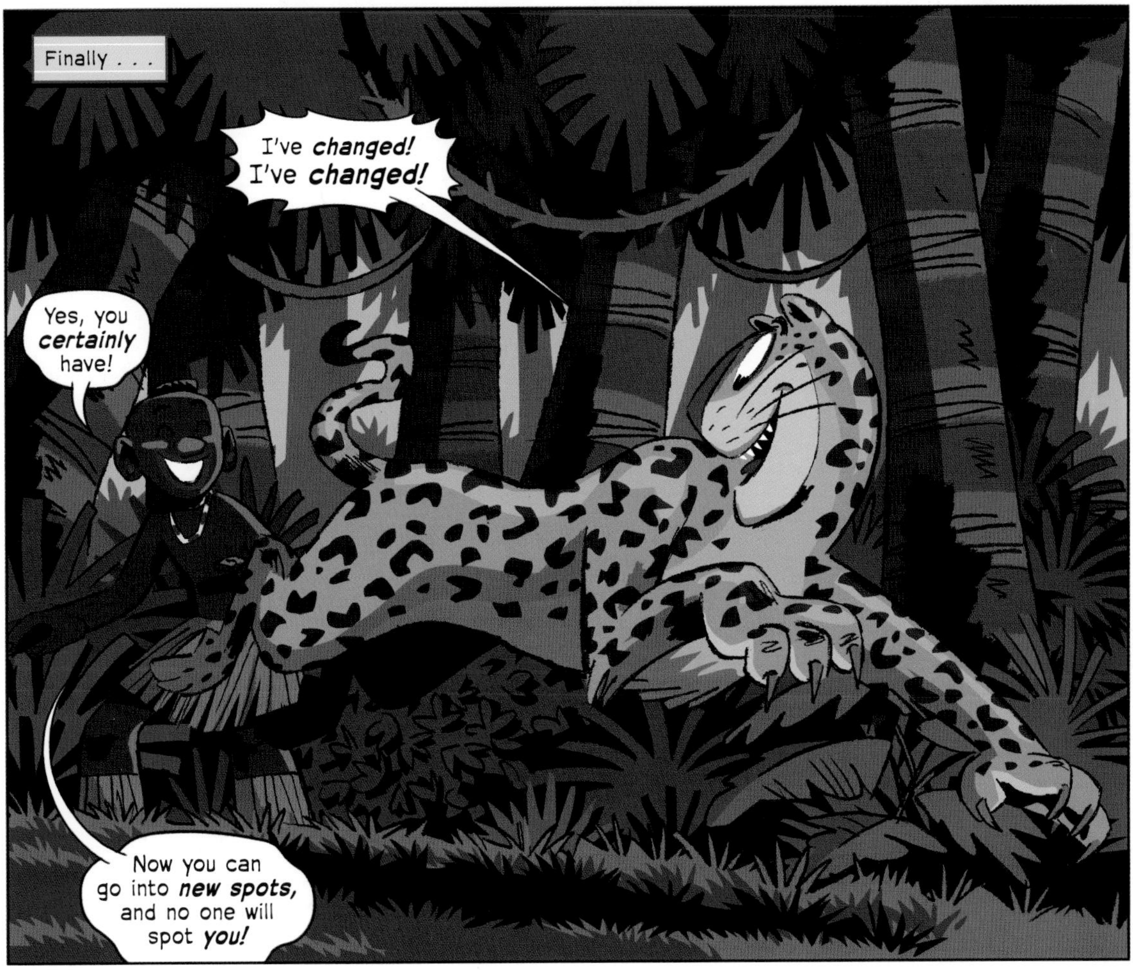
Finally . . .
I've changed! I've changed!
Yes, you certainly have!
Now you can go into new spots, and no one will spot you!

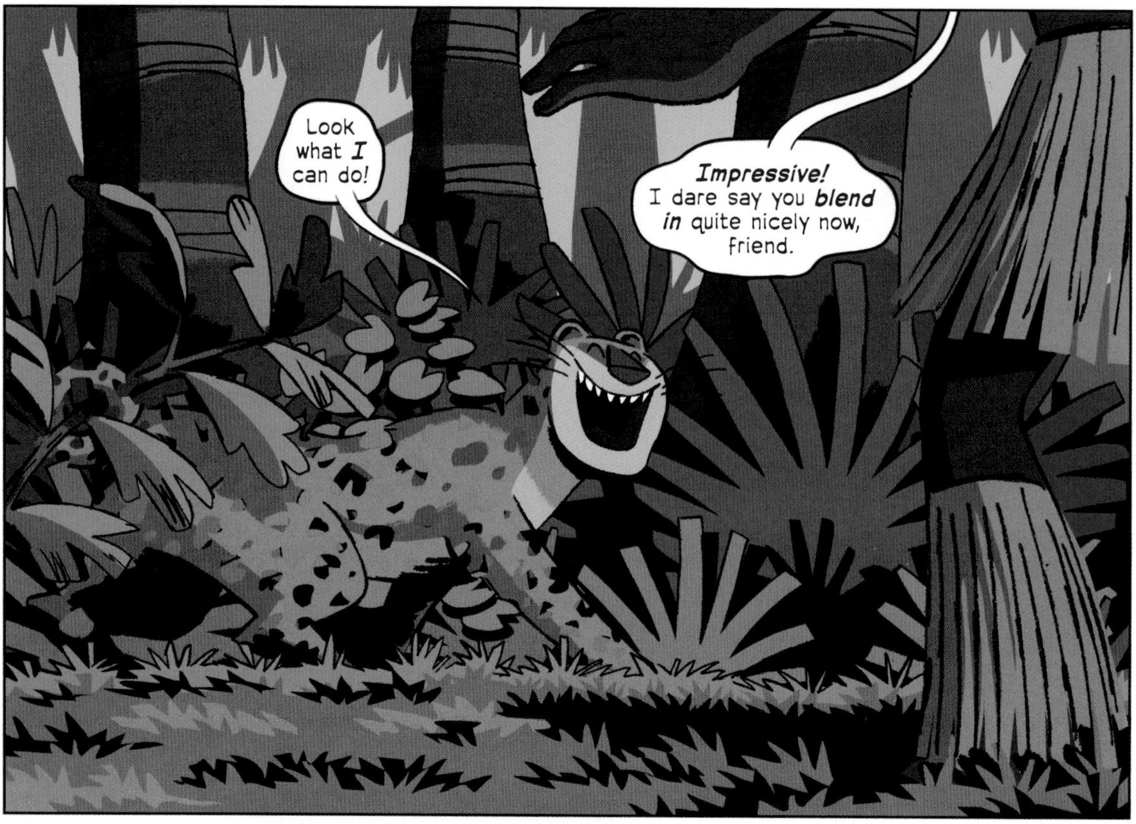
Look what *I* can do!
Impressive! I dare say you ***blend in*** quite nicely now, friend.

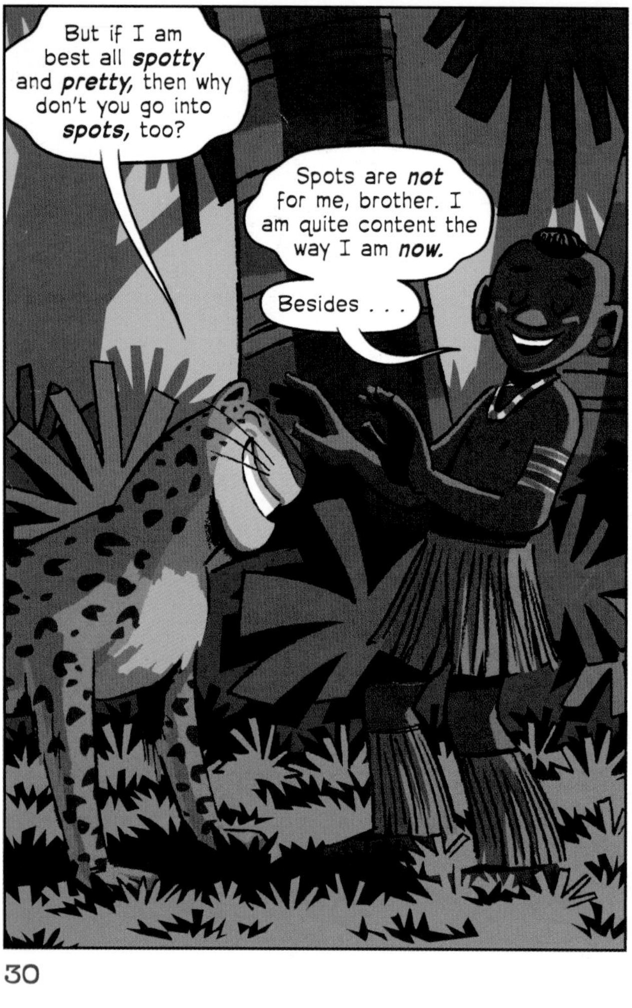
But if I am best all ***spotty*** and ***pretty,*** then why don't you go into ***spots,*** too?
Spots are ***not*** for me, brother. I am quite content the way I am ***now.***
Besides . . .

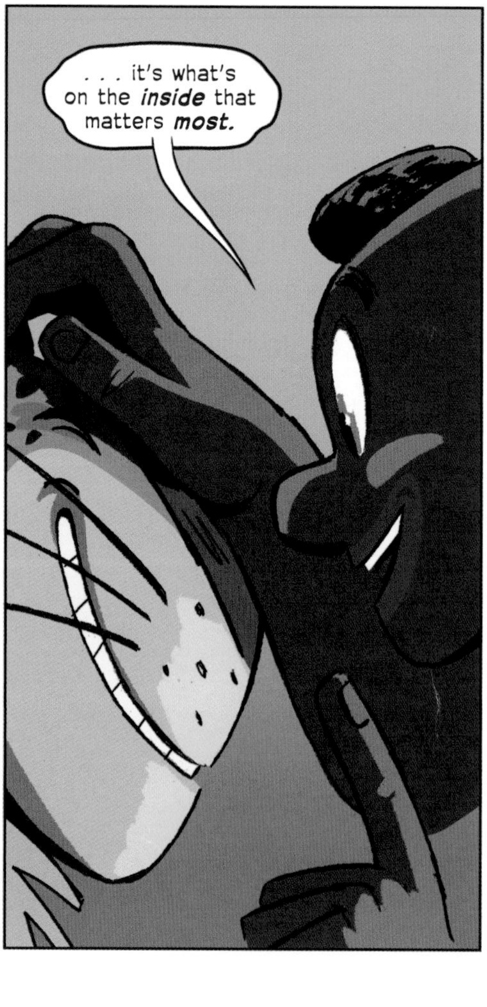
. . . it's what's on the ***inside*** that matters ***most.***

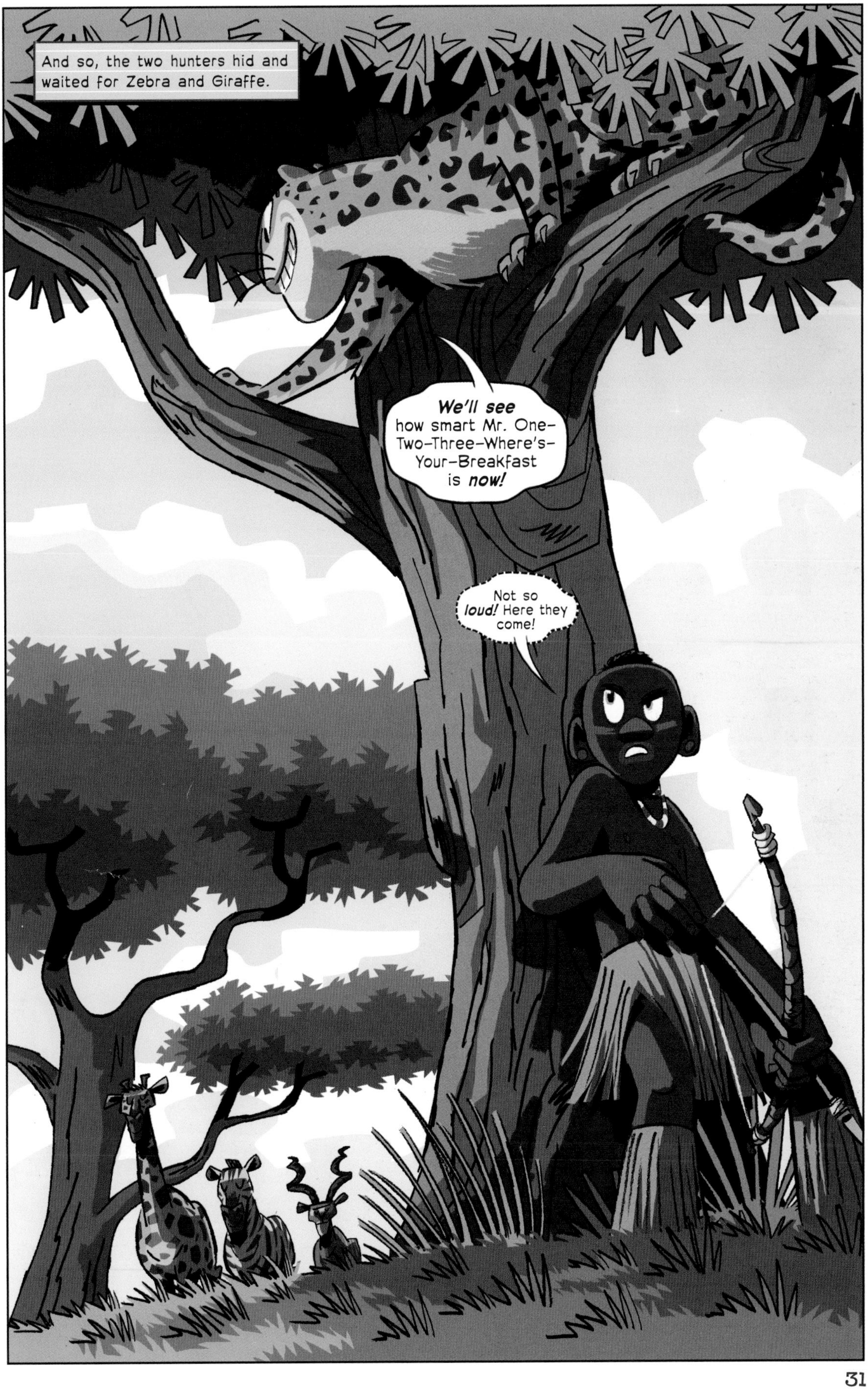
And so, the two hunters hid and waited for Zebra and Giraffe.
We'll see how smart Mr. One-Two-Three-Where's-Your-Breakfast is now!
Not so loud! Here they come!

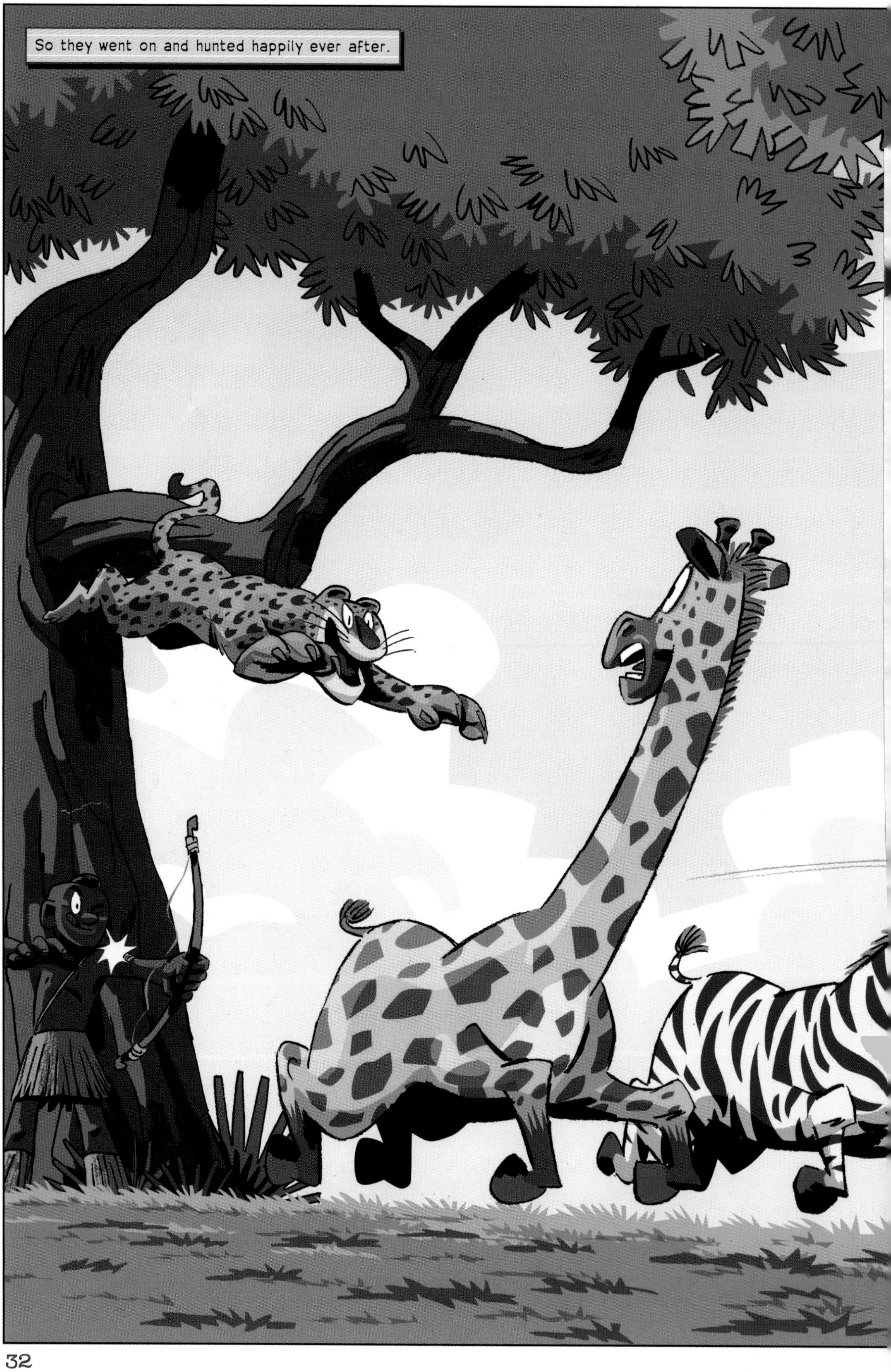
So they went on and hunted happily ever after.

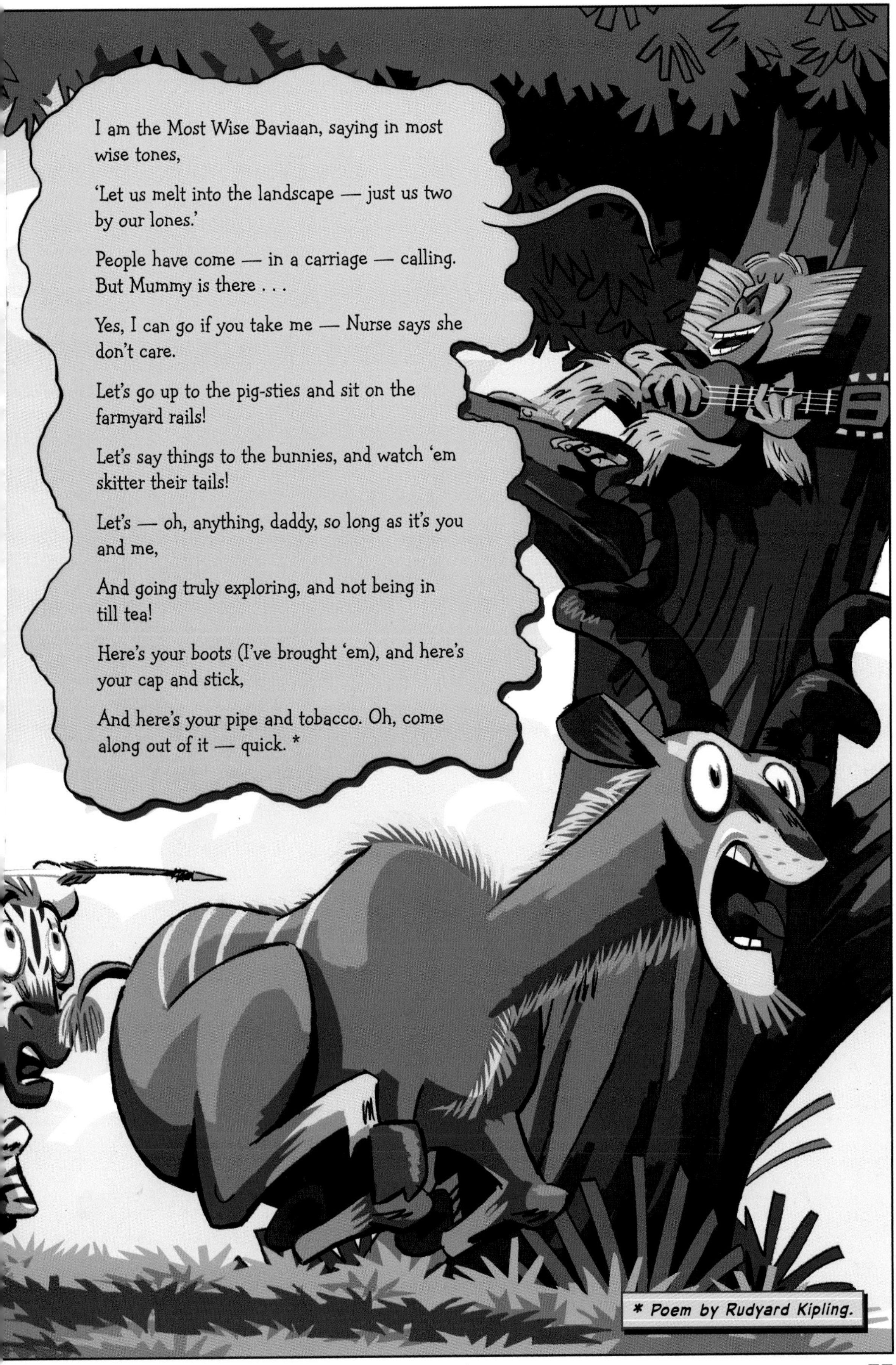

I am the Most Wise Baviaan, saying in most wise tones,
'Let us melt into the landscape — just us two by our lones.'
People have come — in a carriage — calling. But Mummy is there . . .
Yes, I can go if you take me — Nurse says she don't care.
Let's go up to the pig-sties and sit on the farmyard rails!
Let's say things to the bunnies, and watch 'em skitter their tails!
Let's — oh, anything, daddy, so long as it's you and me,
And going truly exploring, and not being in till tea!
Here's your boots (I've brought 'em), and here's your cap and stick,
And here's your pipe and tobacco. Oh, come along out of it — quick. *
* Poem by Rudyard Kipling.

RUDYARD KIPLING
3

CONCLUSION

NEW SPECIMENS:
SUPERBLY-SPOTTED LEOPARD (Fig. A)

THE ETHIOPIAN (Fig. B)
STRIPED ZEBRA (Fig. C)
BANDED KUDU (Fig. D)
SPOTTED GIRAFFE (Fig. E)

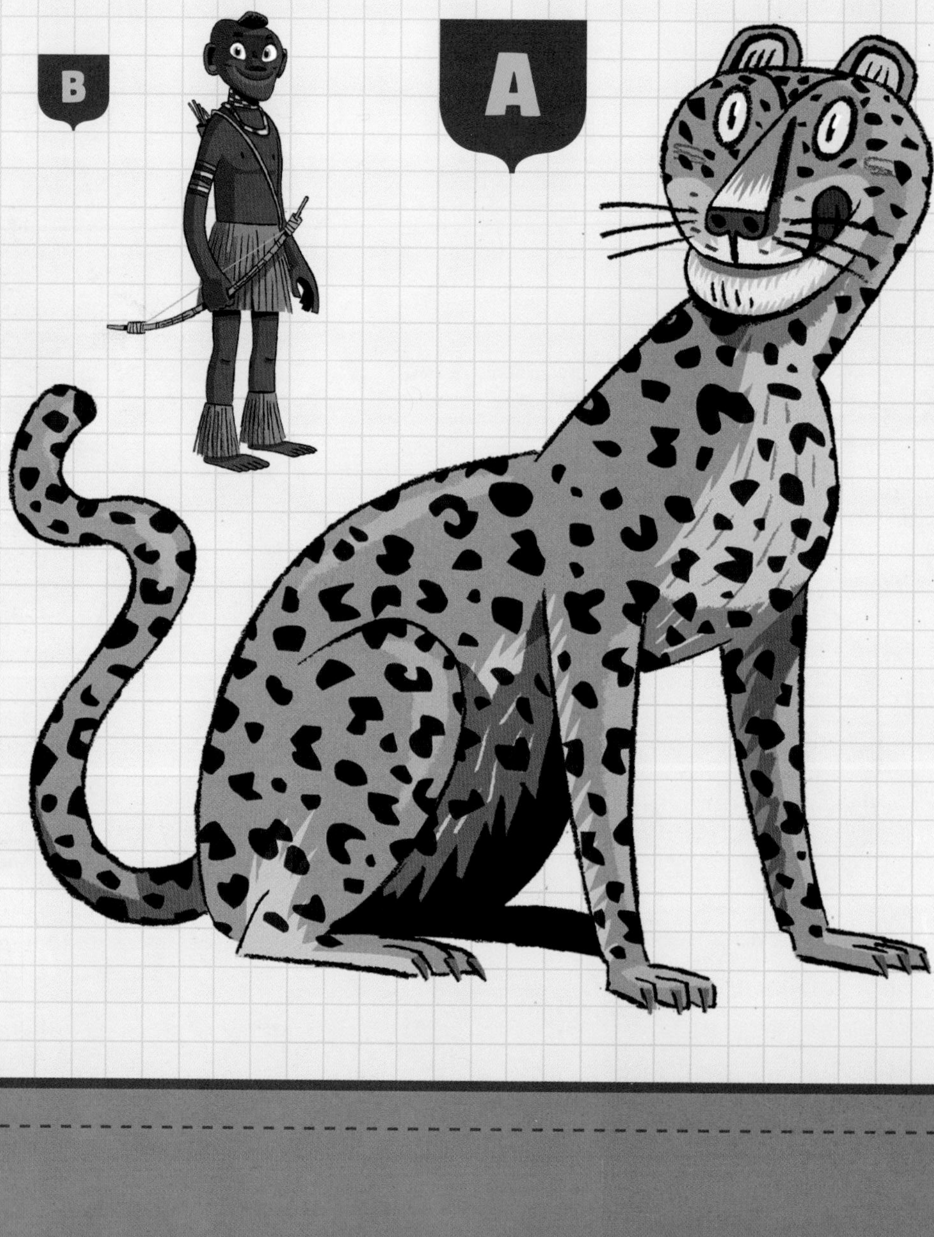

B
A

NOTES:

The leopard is the smallest of the four big cats. Not sure if he suffers from low self-esteem when tiger, lion, or jaguar is around.

Leopards hunt about ninety species of animals, including antelope, rodents, birds, reptiles, and even insects. Not at risk for being labeled "picky eaters."

Leopards can hear five times more sounds than humans. Be thankful that your parents are not leopards.

C

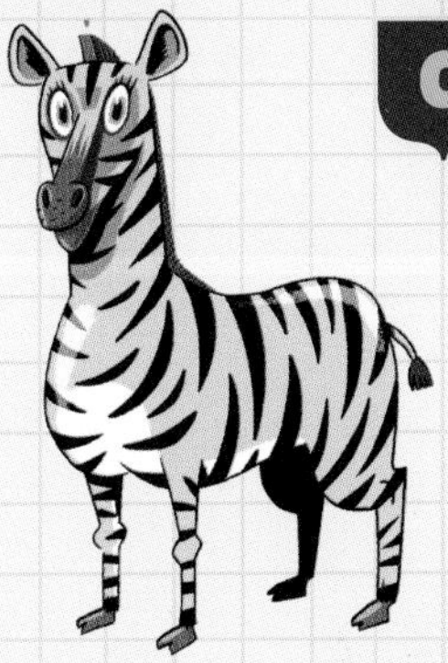

D

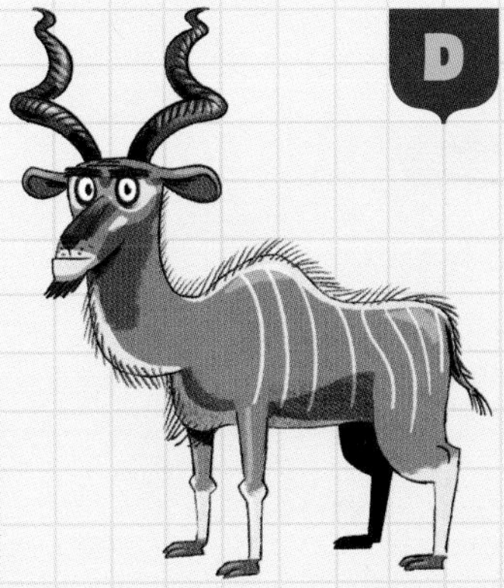

E

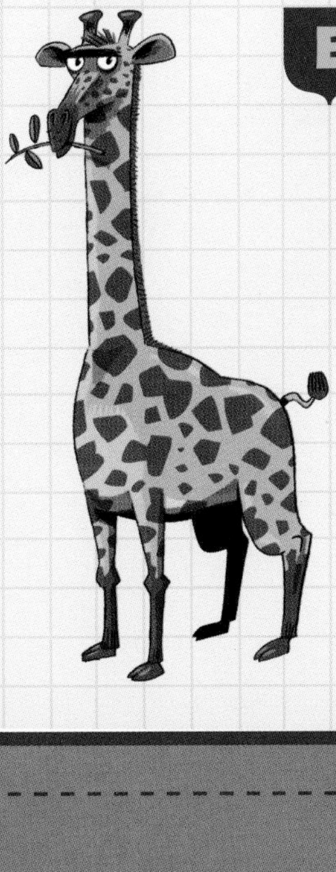

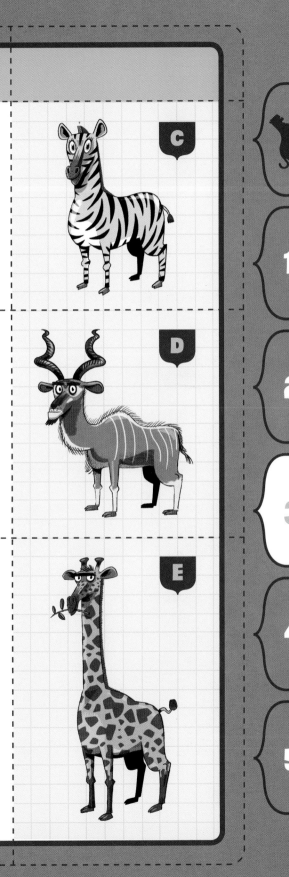

RUDYARD KIPLING
4

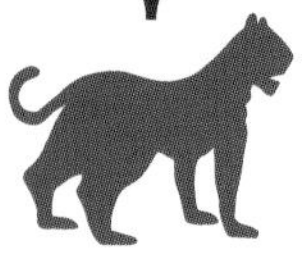

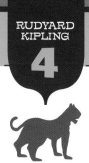

LEARN MORE

Use this handy list of terms and questions to get you started on your own research of the magnificent leopard!

TERMS

aboriginal	(ab-uh-RIJ-uh-nuhl)—being the first of its kind in a region
desperately	(DESS-pur-it-lee)—being beyond or almost beyond hope
excelled	(ek-SELD)—did something extremely well
exclusively	(ek-SKLOO-siv-lee)—completely or wholly
fauna	(FAW-na)—the animal life of a particular area
impressive	(im-PRES-siv)—having the ability to make people think highly of you
insatiable	(in-SAY-shuh-buhl)—impossible to satisfy
migrated	(MYE-grate-ed)—moved from one area to another
procedure	(pruh-SEE-jur)—a way of doing something, especially by a series of steps
relatively	(REL-uh-tiv-lee)—compared with others
splotchy	(SPLAHCH-ee)—spotted

DISCUSSION

1. Why was it important that the animals and the Ethiopian undergo the changes they went through? How did their new appearances help them?

2. The Ethiopian and Leopard went to the Wise Baviaan for advice and help. Do you think he gave them the help they needed? Explain your answer.

3. Kipling ended his field report with a poem, found on page 33. Discuss the poem. Who is the narrator of the poem, and what is it about?

RESEARCH

1. After the animals underwent their changes, they became camouflaged. Research other animals that are camouflaged, choose one, and write a paragraph about it.

2. This is an origin story: it explains how the animals came to look like they do. Write your own animal origin story. For example, explain how snakes came to have no legs or how fish came to have fins.

3. In the story, we do not see Giraffe, Zebra, and Kudu during the first night after their appearance changes. What do you think happened that night? What did they talk about? What did they do? Draw and write a series of panels to show this.

MEET OUR TEAM

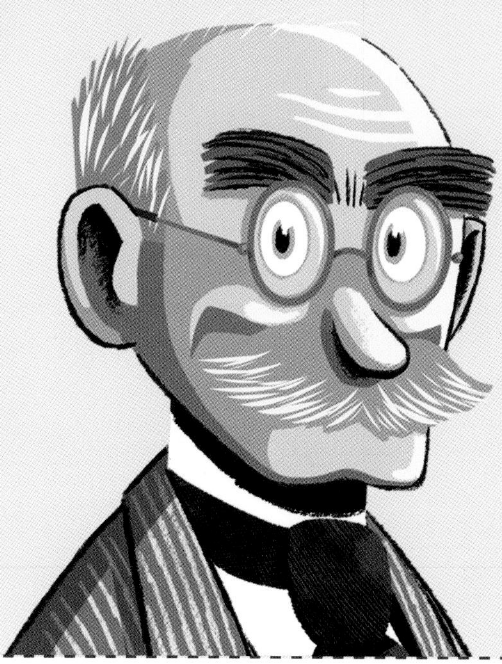

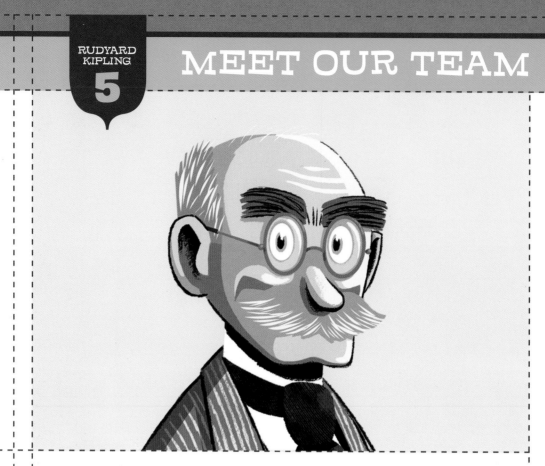

Rudyard Kipling

RUDYARD KIPLING
Founder/Guide

Joseph Rudyard Kipling was born in Bombay, India, on December 30, 1865. He is best known for his short story collections *The Jungle Book*, published in 1894, and *Just So Stories*, published in 1902. He wrote a variety of other short stories, including "Kim" and "The Man Who Would Be King," and many poems. In 1907, he received the Nobel Prize in Literature, becoming the first English-language writer and youngest person to win the award. On January 18, 1936, he died in London at age 70.

SEAN TULIEN
Retelling author

Sean Tulien is a children's book editor living and working in Minnesota. In his spare time, he likes to read, eat sushi, play video games, exercise outdoors, chase after wild animals, listen to loud music, and write books like this one.

PEDRO RODRIGUEZ
Illustrator

Pedro Rodriguez studied illustration at the Fine Arts School in Barcelona, Spain. He has worked in design, marketing, and advertising, creating books, logos, animated films, and music videos. Rodriguez lives in Barcelona with his wife, Gemma, and their daughter, Maya.

JULIE GASSMAN	editor
DONALD LEMKE	managing editor
MICHAEL DAHL	editorial director
BOB LENTZ	designer & letterer
HEATHER KINDSETH	creative director

ALSO AVAILABLE FROM . . .

R
K
RUDYARD KIPLING
EST. 1865

RUDYARD KIPLING'S
HOW THE CAMEL GOT HIS HUMP
THE GRAPHIC NOVEL

RUDYARD KIPLING'S
HOW THE ELEPHANT GOT HIS TRUNK
THE GRAPHIC NOVEL

RUDYARD KIPLING'S
HOW THE RHINOCEROS GOT HIS SKIN
THE GRAPHIC NOVEL

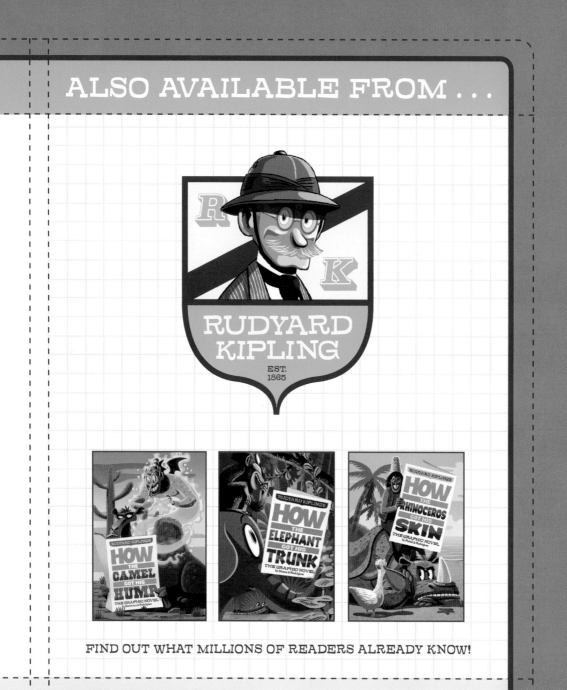

FIND OUT WHAT MILLIONS OF READERS ALREADY KNOW!

STONE ARCH BOOKS™
Published by Stone Arch Books - A Capstone Imprint • 1710 Roe Crest Drive, North Mankato, Minnesota 56003
www.capstonepub.com

Library of Congress Cataloging-in-Publication Data is available on the Library of Congress website.
Library binding: 978-1-4342-3223-6 • Paperback: 978-1-4342-3881-8

Summary: A leopard finds a way to get some spots in this graphic retelling of Rudyard Kipling's classic tale.

Printed in the United States of America in North Mankato, Minnesota.
022013 007186R